William Livingston Alden

Shooting Stars as Observed from the Sixth Column of the Times

William Livingston Alden

Shooting Stars as Observed from the Sixth Column of the Times

ISBN/EAN: 9783337411466

Printed in Europe, USA, Canada, Australia, Japan

Cover: Foto ©Andreas Hilbeck / pixelio.de

More available books at **www.hansebooks.com**

SHOOTING STARS

AS OBSERVED FROM

THE "SIXTH COLUMN" OF THE TIMES

BY
W. L. ALDEN

———————

NEW YORK
G. P. PUTNAM'S SONS.
1878.

CONTENTS.

LIST OF ILLUSTRATIONS.

SHOOTING STARS.

FROM time immemorial the shooting star has ministered to the happiness of lovers. When two hearts that beat as one, with, of course, the usual accompanying organs, limbs, and clothes, are seated on the piazza in the quiet of a summer evening, a kiss may properly be exchanged whenever a meteor is seen. Upon this point all the authorities from ANACREON to the *Sun*, are unanimous. SOCRATES, indeed, went so far as to hold that nature provides shooting stars and bridges for the sole benefit of lovers, for in the eighteenth book of the " Memoriabilia," he is reported to have said to ALCIBIADES, in the course of an argument for the existence of the gods, based upon the evidences of design in nature : " You, yourself, O, ALCIBIADES, know that if you or I cross a bridge while sleighing, or discover a meteor in the firmament, we consecrate a kiss to Zeus. Why, then, did Zeus create bridges and meteors unless in order that you and I should —" At this moment, as XENOPHON informs us, XANTIPPE entered, and the sage, suddenly recollecting that he had an appointment down town, abruptly dismissed his class in philosophy. We do not, however, need the authority of the ancients to prove the existence of a custom familiar to us all. This custom has naturally trained the youth of both sexes to great skill in the detection of meteors. It is not very long ago that a young lady of Oshkosh, while sitting with her betrothed on the back piazza, pointed out to him thirty-six meteors in the course of a single hour, and subsequently permitted her astronomical enthusiasm to lead her to insist that the flashes of a lantern in the hands of a brakeman engaged in coupling together a long freight train, were so many additional meteors of a peculiarly interesting type.

Vassar College, as every one knows, contains a vast collection of girls of all sizes, weights, and colors of hair. Those who control the institution have an intense horror of the co-education of the sexes, and permit no male students to cross the threshold, or even to enter the front gate of the college. The girls are strictly secluded from all young men, and the members of the Faculty are united in a determined disbelief in the existence of all cousins and brothers. It has just been announced that since the 14th of September last the Vassar students have sighted two hundred meteors. Now, in view of the utter dearth of young men at Vassar, and the known uses of meteors, the question arises, How were these two hundred meteors observed? The question is one which comes home with tremendous force to the parents of the Vassar young ladies, and which cannot be lightly set aside by the Vassar Faculty, who are directly responsible for the method in which the students pursue the study of astronomy.

Of course, every one knows that when girls are

bent upon dancing, and young men are absolutely unattainable, a select number of girls are frequently temporarily transformed into theoretical young men, by simply tying handkerchiefs around their left arms. It may be pretended that a similar expedient has been employed to aid the Vassar young ladies in observing meteors. The Faculty may as well understand at once that no such flimsy pretense will satisfy the public. Theoretical young men may be made use of amid the excitement of a dance, but no young lady, no matter if she were to "make believe" with even greater skill than the "Marchioness," would be able to convince herself that another young lady with a handkerchief around her left arm could constitute an efficient aid to the observation of meteors. The two hundred meteors lately observed at Vassar were never observed under such conditions. The girls may have sat in pairs on the back piazza, with a pretended view to meteors, but if so, their observations were confined to dresses, bonnets, and other feminine phenomena, and not to the starry heavens.

Are we, then, to assume either that the astronomical observatory of Vassar College has recently added three or four dozen young men to the rest of its apparatus, or that the alleged two hundred meteors were never really seen, but were the invention of a number of ingenious and somewhat too imaginative young ladies? Fortunately, we are not compelled to accept either of these hypotheses. To suppose that the Vassar Faculty have fitted up the observatory with young men, would be to impute to them a reckless determination to enforce the study of astronomy at the sacrifice of the very principle upon which Vassar College is founded, while to suppose that young ladies would profess to see meteors when none were visible, is to charge them with the one offense of which the sex is never guilty—a want of veracity.

If, then, we concede that the two hundred meteors were really observed by the Vassar astronomical class without the aid of any additions to the usual apparatus of the observatory, we are brought face to face with the question, who is the

Vassar Professor of Astronomy? He may be venerable in point of years, and absolutely full of science, but can he expect to be believed when he pretends that he teaches the young ladies the uses of meteors simply from pure love of science? Astronomers are fond of taxing human credulity, and it must be confessed that they usually succeed. For example, the pretense that they have discovered the names of the stars by aid of instruments and calculations is almost an insult to common sense, and yet it is universally believed. There is, however, a limit beyond which the boldest astronomical person cannot safely go, and the Vassar Professor of Astronomy will pass this limit if he attempts any such defense as that just mentioned. Possibly, he can explain the whole affair in a way that will be perfectly satisfactory to every one; but if he cannot, let him at least be frank and truthful. It will then be time to consider whether the study of shooting stars should be any longer pursued at Vassar. It is, of course, a fascinating study, but it can be pursued as a postgraduate study, under the direction of an accomplished cousin, with far better results than can attend the instruction of a class of immature girls by an ancient scientific person.

THE TOMBIGBEE INCIDENT.

THE Town of Clayville, situated some thirty miles from the mouth of the Tombigbee River, is at present greatly excited over the departure of the local colored minister, who recently started down the river on board a large and strongly-built colored sister, and who has not since been heard from. The circumstances attending the minister's departure were peculiar, and their publication may, perhaps, aid the recovery of the intrepid, though unintentional, voyager.

The minister in question was of the Colored Baptist persuasion, and was famed throughout the Tombigbee Valley for his skill as a baptizer, as well as for his ability as a preacher. There is no doubt that he was a fearless and conscientious man. Instead of maintaining that politic silence on the subject of chickens which many colored ministers insist is absolutely necessary, in order to avoid chilling the fervor of their hearers, this particular minister never hesitated to declare that a right of property in chickens existed, and that it should be respected in certain cases, and to a greater or less extent, by all honest men, especially during the season when hams are readily accessible. This bold doctrine, instead of injuring his popularity, actually increased the respect in which he was held by his congregation, and gave him much prominence among his ministerial brethren.

Among the colored ladies of Clayville was one who had long desired to submit to the rite of baptism, but who was deterred by a nervous dread of drowning and by a strong repugnance to the inevitable wetting which is inseparable from the rite. Scores of times this estimable lady had determined to be baptized at the next available opportunity, but at the last moment her courage always failed her. In the days prior to emancipation, she had been the slave of a Clayville planter, and she still retained a warm affection for the young master whom she had nursed in his infancy. Not very long ago this young man called to see her, and to him she lamented the lack of courage which shut her out from baptism. Whether he was influenced by genuine kindness, or by a wicked spirit of irreverence, will perhaps never be known; but the advice which he gave his confiding nurse was the cause of the painful tragedy which followed.

The young man professed to be surprised that the new safety baptismal robe, invented, as he alleged, by Rev. Dr. PAUL BOYTON, of New York, had not yet been adopted by the colored Baptists of the South. He said that he had one of these robes in his possession, and that the wearer would not only be safe against any possibility of drowning, but also against the possibility of getting wet. Moreover, it could be worn underneath the usual white cotton robe, without any danger of detection. The overjoyed candidate for baptism enthusiastically accepted the young man's advice and his offer of the robe, and she immediately sent word to the minister that she would certainly be ready for baptism the very next Sunday.

There was such a general distrust of the sister's

courage that the colored people all assembled on the bank of the Tombigbee on the next day, confident that her courage would fail, and that she would endeavor to escape from the hands of the minister. The particular part of the river selected for the ceremony was comparatively shallow, but the current was swift, and a little lower down the depth was at least ten feet. In fact, the minister, in spite of his skill, had once lost a convert, who was carried away by the current, and who, on being rescued, promptly went over to the Methodists. The timid candidate was an unusually large woman, and was certain to tax the minister's strength severely; so that there could be little doubt that the ceremony would be one of unusual interest.

The sister arrived at the appointed time, looking even larger than usual, and walking with much difficulty. The minister took her by the hand, and she fearlessly descended into the water. All went well until she reached the depth of about four feet, when she suddenly fell upon her back, and to the astonishment of the spectators, floated on the sur-

face of the water. The excitement at this unprecedented event was tremendous, and the air was
filled with enthusiastic shouts. The minister's
face, however, wore a troubled expression. He
towed the unaccountably buoyant sister out into
deeper water, and attempted to place her on her
feet. The attempt proved impracticable, and he
then tried to immerse her without changing her
position. In spite of all his efforts, he could not
force her under, and the spectators who witnessed
the struggle soon became convinced that she was
bewitched. They counseled the minister to exor-
cise the evil one by whom she was evidently possessed, with an axe, and volunteered to supply him
with heavy weights wherewith to securely sink
her. That devoted man, however, refused their
counsel, and persisted in his effort to immerse the
sister without the aid of weights. Finally he
threw his whole weight upon her, and in a
moment the current swept the pair beyond their
depth.

In spite of the danger of his situation, the minister's cheek did not blanch. With great presence of mind he seated himself comfortably upon the floating sister, and, waving a farewell to his congregation, began to sing a cheerful hymn. The current steadily carried him on at the rate of at least six miles an hour, and in a short time his weeping congregation was left out of sight and hearing. Without oars or sails he was unable to navigate the sister to the shore, and there is every reason to suppose that before the next morning he was far out on the Gulf of Mexico.

Captains of vessels navigating the Gulf have been requested to keep a sharp lookout for a colored sister in a Boyton life-saving dress, carrying a colored minister on her deck. Let us hope that he will soon be picked up. He has now been afloat five days without provisions or water, and must be beginning to feel the need of refreshment. Of course, any Captain who may rescue him will not ask for a reward, but if he tows the sister into port he can claim salvage to a large amount, and libel her in the nearest admiralty court.

A SPANISH SMUGGLER.

HERE is another of those occasions which cause the conscientious journalist to wish that he had never been born. The cold world little thinks of the terrible cost at which it is sometimes furnished with the news of the day. There are events of which the public must be apprised, but which cannot be told without lacerating the feelings of the earnest and sensitive narrator. An event of this nature has just happened in Madrid. It would be cowardly and dishonest to suppress it. Moreover, the story comes directly from the State Department at Washington, and it is by no means certain that its suppression would not be an act of rebellion. Let us, then, go forward boldly and discharge a painful duty without murmuring.

The Spaniard is not usually thought to possess

inventive genius. Among all the important inventions which have been made since the union of Castile and Arragon, the art of " walking Spanish" is the only one which has been attributed to the Spanish intellect. But there has at last appeared a Spaniard who is clearly entitled to be ranked as one of the ablest of living inventors, and it is the history of his invention which must now be laid before the public.

The city of Madrid is, as every one knows, a walled city. It is not, however, generally known that nearly all merchandise which is brought into the city has to pay a special duty, no matter if it is an imported article which has been already taxed at a Spanish custom-house. This is the case with petroleum. It is heavily taxed when it enters Spanish territory and is again taxed still more heavily when it enters Madrid. Hence a great temptation to smuggle is offered to those who supply petroleum to the inhabitants of Madrid, and were the Spaniards an ingenious people, they would devote so much attention to smuggling that they would have no time left to celebrate their annual revolutions.

In the outskirts of Madrid Don JOSE DE ANTI-QUEDAD Y VUELTA-ABAJO possesses a charming villa with extensive grounds and numerous outbuildings. He has long been known as an extremely benevolent man, always ready to approve of any act of charity, and eager to point out fields of philanthropic usefulness to other people. About six months ago he announced that the condition of the babies of Madrid filled him with grief, and that he was determined to alleviate their sufferings. In the course of an elaborate essay, which he published in pamphlet form, he demonstrated that infants could not be reared without artificial aid in a crowded city. He claimed that no matter how excellent might be the intentions of the mothers of Madrid, they could not furnish their infants with desirable board because their systems were affected in a deleterious manner by the unwholesome atmosphere of the city. As for the auxiliary bottle, he condemned it with much fierceness. "Never

with my consent," said this excellent man, ". shall
the youth of Madrid undergo the humiliation of
the unsympathetic and unsatisfactory bottle."
The true solution of the problem how to feed the
babies of Madrid was, however, a simple one in his
estimation. He announced that he would keep
constantly on hand a large supply of unexceptionable nurses at his suburban estate. There is some
difficulty in translating his exact descriptive phrase
into English, but perhaps it will suffice to say that
his nurses were warranted to be able to supply the
wants of the Madrid infants without the aid of
bottles. In short, they were to be self-acting, pe-
rennial, and inexhaustible, and with their assistance
Don JOSE DE ANTIQUEDAD Y VUELTA-ABAJO undertook to supply Madrid with pure Naranjos County
—well! at all events the Madrid infants were to
be fed.

A few weeks later and Don JOSE advertised that
his establishment was in complete order, and that
his nurses would enter the city daily to wait upon
their customers. Apparently, he had a great many

patrons, for a few days later a procession of at
least a dozen extremely plump Spanish women,
whose very appearance was sufficient to awaken
the hunger of the most dainty infant, made their
appearance at the city gate. The custom-house
officers gazed at them with respect and admiration,
and warmly congratulated the Madrid infants upon
their good fortune. The praises of the benevolent
Don JOSE were in every mouth. The local press
published frequent leading articles asserting that
the local infants were thriving to an extent hitherto unknown, and hinting that the grand regalia of
the Order of St. Intimidad had been given to many
men who deserved it less than did the beneficent
Don JOSE. For three months the procession of
nurses entered the city at morning, noon, and
night, and grew in numbers, until it was no unusual thing for sixty women to present themselves
at the gate at one and the same time.

On the 4th day of March last, it happened
that a new custom-house officer, Lieut. COLORADO
MADURO, who was on duty at the Zarzuela gate

when the noon procession of nurses made its appearance. He was a thoughtful, intelligent man, but he was not popular with the small-boys of Madrid. Just as the leading nurse, Senora Rosa Concha, entered the city, a stone, thrown at the officer, missed its mark and smote the nurse in the region of the lungs. To the officer's great astonishment, the blow produced a hollow metallic sound which at once awakened his suspicions. Without a moment's delay, Lieut. MADURO called out a file of soldiers, and arresting every nurse, sent for two female searchers and ordered them to do their duty. Twenty minutes later sixty exceptionally thin and sad-looking women were marched to the city prison, and one hundred and twenty cans, of a curious hemispheric shape, filled with petroleum, were lying heaped together where the female-searchers had thrown them.

DON JOSE DE ANTIQUEDAD Y VUELTA-ABAJO was thus discovered to be an impostor. He had not furnished a single Madrid infant with pure Naranjos county—well, food. He was not a philanthropist, and he cared neither for nurses nor children. He was, however, an audacious and ingenious smuggler, and the long success of his artifice has so overthrown Spanish faith in woman, that none but the thinnest and most level of the sex can pass a Spanish custom-house without undergoing the most rigid scrutiny.

CHRISTMAS AT WINDSOR CASTLE.

IT is rarely that the public obtains a glimpse of the private life of monarchs. They are never seen by their subjects except in full dress, and equipped with what New England people are accustomed to call " company manners." Thus only the outer shell, so to speak, of the German Emperor or the British Queen is known to their people. We all know, of course, that the Emperor is mortal, and hence must at times put on a night-shirt, and that even Queen VICTORIA must do up her back hair on going to bed, just as though she were an ordinary British matron, but even the most enterprising special correspondent is unable to describe these imperial and royal acts from his own personal knowledge. We of this generation are, however, exceptionally fortunate in regard to the good and gracious Queen of England. In the

2

Life of the Prince Consort, which is virtually written by her, we are taken into the interior of the
royal palace and admitted to the privacy of the
royal family.   It is safe to say that the present
generation is acquainted with the royal family of
England more intimately than any previous generation has been acquainted with any other royal
household.   The Queen's description of a Christmas at Windsor Castle is of especial interest just
at present, and as it has not yet been published in
this country, a summary of it, obtained from advance
sheets, may interest the public.

The particular Christmas referred to was that
of the year 1849.   Especial efforts were made to
render that occasion one of unusual domestic
felicity.   The Prince Consort had said, "Mother,
we must have a first-class shindy for the children
this time," and the amiable Queen had answered,
"ALBERT, we will just make things whoop."   Accordingly, an immense amount of presents was
provided, and the royal parents determined to personally superintend the filling of the stockings—a

duty which ordinarily devolved upon Lord JOHN RUSSELL.

"On Christmas eve"—so we are told—"the Queen remarked, 'ALBERT, I believe I will hang up my own stocking, and you shall fill it.' The Prince, with that excellent good sense which never failed him, replied: 'My dear, it will not do. There must be a limit to the size of stockings. Hang up a pillow-case, if you want to, or even a bolster, but remember that I can't afford to sit up all night filling unlimited space with expensive presents.'" Her Majesty thereupon changed her mind, and full of anxiety to make her husband happy, volunteered to fill the stockings herself, so that the Prince could go to bed early.

During the evening the children were, of course, unusually wide awake. Half a dozen times was the Queen compelled to go to the foot of the front stairs and order them to go instantly to sleep. Threats were even necessary before they could be quieted, and the Prince Consort was finally obliged to remark, "If you children let me hear one more word out of you this night I shall come up stairs with a club." Whereupon the children ceased their uproar, and by ten o'clock were soundly asleep.

"It was the wish of the Prince," continues the narrative, "to sleep in the nursery with the children, so that he could see them open their stockings in the morning." As the Queen desired to hang a portrait of herself over the Prince's bed, as a pleasant surprise for him, she was compelled to wait until he was sound asleep. At 1 o'clock A. M. her Majesty stealthily entered the nursery, with seven well-filled stockings hanging on her arm. Just as she crossed the threshold two of the stockings slipped from her grasp and fell with considerable noise, but without awakening the children or interrupting Prince ALBERT's gentle snore. It so happened that the Duke of Wellington, when filling the stove for the night, had inadvertently left a coal-scuttle in the middle of the floor, and the Queen, not dreaming of such an obstacle, fell over it with a loud crash. The

Prince of Wales moved uneasily in his bed, but continued to sleep soundly, as did all the other children and their gracious father. Fortunately, the Queen fell on the stockings, which were largely stuffed with molasses candy of a yielding nature, and so sustained no injury. Finally the stockings were hung in their proper place and the Queen proceeded to place her portrait on the wall over the Prince Consort's head. To do this it was necessary for her to stand on the bed. Now to walk over a well-filled bed in a dimly-lighted room is a difficult operation, and it thus happened that the Queen stepped somewhat heavily upon the Prince. It was the last straw that broke his princely slumbers, and also flattened his ribs. In those circumstances, instead of betraying impatience, he merely groaned heavily and exclaimed: "Go on: mash in the rest of them! Get the Princess of Cambridge to help you. Let joy be unconfined!" and further language to that effect. So moved was her Majesty by his suffering and fortitude that she burst into tears and nearly fell upon him, thereby eliciting a yell of terror. This woke up the children, who fancying that morning had arrived, clutched their stockings and began the joyful uproar which in every happy home ushers in the blessed Christmas morn.

"There was not a closed eye in the castle from that moment until breakfast time"— continues the writer of the narrative. When the royal pair met at the breakfast table they were as tired as if they had attended a ball. The Prince withdrew to his own apartment as soon as the meal was ended, and played on the flute for several hours—an exercise which always calmed his mind and fitted other persons to bear the prospect of his early death; while the Queen signed three death-warrants with a firmness which she had never before displayed. Before night every one of the children was writhing in the agonies of colic, and the court physician had expressed the opinion that the Prince Consort's ribs were in a most precarious condition. "It was then decided," adds the royal biographer—"that the custom of hanging up stockings should be abolished in the precincts of the castle, a resolution which has been strictly kept."

We thus see from this pleasing glimpse of England's royal household that Queens and Princes are much like other people. It is impossible to avoid honoring her Majesty's kindly ways, and the Prince's fortitude under suffering. No royal Briton can read this touching narrative without tears, and without asking himself the solemn question, how much the Queen weighed in 1849.

SERENADING IN ST. LOUIS.

THERE are two young men in St. Louis who at the present time are so diversified as to their surfaces with brown paper and sticking-plaster that they might readily be mistaken for Bulgarian Christians who had just been receiving a good deal of protection from the Russian Cossacks. They do not bear their plasters with resignation, for they are not good young men. The testimony of large numbers of St. Louisians proves that the two young men in question frequent bar-rooms and quarrel in the public streets, make night hideous with uproar, and play upon musical instruments, like the beasts that perish. Their wounds and bruises are a just retribution for their misdeeds, and they deserve no sympathy whatever.

There is a young lady in St. Louis, living in a nice suburban cottage, with whom both these young

men are madly in love. Being thus rivals, they
naturally hate each other, and not very long ago
discussed their respective fitness for the young
lady's hand in the public street, with the use of
much strong Western language and the display of
revolvers and knives. On this occasion, however,
they did not actually assault one another, but each
young man, after having solemnly pledged himself
to cut the other into fine slices at their next meeting, went his way in search of privacy and rum.
Two days later they met in a bar-room, and, instead of carrying out their sanguinary intentions,
they fell upon their respective necks and vowed
eternal friendship. They decided that the young
lady was not an object of sufficient importance to
be permitted to envelop their newborn friendship in
a cloud of suspicion and jealousy, and they resolved that, renouncing all claims to her affection,
they would live for each other only. They mutually promised never to see or to think of her again,
and finally separated on apparently the very
warmest terms of friendship. It was noticed,

2*

however, by several unimpeachable witnesses, that
as soon as they had put a large and opaque German between them, they stoutly shook their
clenched fists and smiled in a ghastly and sarcastic
manner. The truth is, their reconciliation was a
hollow mockery, and their pretended abandonment
of the young lady was an act of premeditated de-
ceit and treachery. Each desired to occupy un-
molested the field of courtship, and believed that
he had outwitted his rival and rendered him no
longer dangerous.

It has been remarked that among their other
vices was that of playing upon wind instruments.
One of them played the cornet, while the other
was habitually addicted to the bassoon. While
the latter instrument is not so immediately fatal to
the helpless listener as is the cornet, it is much
more weakening to the mind, and the agonies
which it inflicts are more prolonged and painful.
It was the intention of these young men to serenade the object of their devotion on the very evening of the day when they formed their hollow and

insincere alliance, and each of them presumed that he had secured a monopoly of her midnight ears. But as BURNS has remarked, the best schemes of policy devised, either by mice or conciliatory Presidents, frequently go "aglee," which, being interpreted, means "to eternal smash." And such was the destiny of the serenading schemes of the two bad young men.

The young lady's bedroom was in the northeast corner of the second story of her house, and the house stood in the midst of a large and beautiful lawn. Precisely at 11:15 P. M. the young man with the cornet opened upon her under her north window with the pathetic air of "Silver Threads among the Gold;" but almost at the same moment he metaphorically smote his breast, for he heard under the east window the loud bassoon in the act of wrestling with the "Arkansas Traveler." In these circumstances few young men would have subordinated a thirst for immediate vengeance to their artistic pride, but the two bad young men, while mentally resolving to kill one another in the near future, were equally resolved not to permit their devotion to music to be interrupted. They threw their whole beings into their respective instruments, and the blare of the cornet mingled in wild confusion with the groans of the bassoon. The young lady, who was a girl of much spirit and practical common sense, very soon began to throw things, but neither water, old shoes, nor crockery could move the determined serenaders. They continued to blow until each had finished his allotted tune, after which, with a fierceness rivaling that of the wild cats of the nocturnal back fence, and with oaths at which the most hardened cat would have shuddered, they poised their musical weapons over their heads and rushed simultaneously to the combat.

The bassoon is longer than the cornet, but the latter has greater weight and hardness, and the two combatants were thus very equally matched as to their weapons. They fought with frightful energy, and were encouraged by the cheerful comments of the young lady, who, like the Blessed Damosel, leaned from her window, and with great impartiality urged each one to "everlastingly lay out" the other. The bassoon fell with resounding blows upon the head of the cornet player, and the sharp edge of the bell of the cornet gashed the bassoon-player's face and lacerated his knuckles. Neither would yield, and had not the young lady's father risen from his couch, and with great presence of mind checked the further effusion of blood by firing upon the rivals with his shot-gun, the fight would probably have had a fatal termination. As it was, as soon as their legs became overweighted with buckshot, the two young men laid down their weapons, and were soon after carried by the police to the nearest hospital for repairs.

This story teaches us how blessed a thing it is for two young men to serenade the same young woman at the same time, whereby their instruments are certain to be ruined, and they themselves are very likely to be permanently spoiled.

A PATENTED CHILD.

THE town of Sussex, Pennsylvania, has lately been profoundly stirred by an extraordinary and romantic lawsuit. The case was an entirely novel one, and no precedent bearing upon it is to be found in the common or statute law. While it is necessarily a matter of great interest to the legal profession, its romantic side cannot fail to attract the attention of persons of all ages and every kind of sex. In fact, it is destined to be one of the most celebrated cases in the annals of American jurisprudence.

Some time last winter a lady whom we will call Mrs. Smith, who kept a boarding-house in Sussex, took her little girl, aged four, with her to make a call on Mrs. Brown, her near neighbor. Mrs. Brown was busy in her kitchen, where she received her visitor with her usual cordiality. There was a large fire blazing in the stove, and while the ladies were excitedly discussing the new bonnet of the local Methodist minister's wife, the little girl incautiously sat down on the stove-hearth. She was instantly convinced that the hearth was exceedingly hot, and on loudly bewailing the fact, was rescued by her mother and carried home for medical treatment. A few days later Mrs. Smith burst in great excitement into the room of a young law student, who was one of her boarders, and with tears and lamentations disclosed to him the fact that her child was indelibly branded with the legend, "Patented. 1872." These words in raised letters had happened to occupy just that part of the stove-hearth on which the child had seated herself, and being heated nearly to red-heat they had reproduced themselves on the surface of the unfortunate child.

The law student entered into the mother's sorrow with much sympathy, but after he had in some degree calmed her mind he informed her that a breach of law had been committed. "Your child,"

he remarked, " has never been patented, but she is
marked 'Patented. 1872.' This is an infringement of the statute. You falsely represent by
that brand that a child for whom no patent has
issued is patented. This false representation is
forgery, and subjects you to the penalty made and
provided for that crime."

Mrs. Smith was, as may be supposed, greatly
alarmed at hearing this statement, and her first im-
pulse was to beg the young man to save her from
a convict's cell. With a gravity suited to the occasion, he explained the whole law of patents. He
told her that had she desired to patent the child,
she should have either constructed a model of it or
prepared accurate drawings, with specifications
showing distinctly what parts of the child she
claimed to have invented. This model or these
drawings she should have forwarded to the Patent
Office, and she would then have received in due
time a patent—provided, of course, the child was
really patentable—and would have been authorized
to label it " Patented." " Unfortunately," he

pursued, "it is now too late to take this course, and we must boldly claim that a patent was issued, but that the record was destroyed during the recent fire in the Patent Office."

This suggestion cheered the spirits of Mrs. Smith, but they were again dashed by the further remarks of the young man. He reminded her that the child might find it very inconvenient to be patented. "If we claim"—he went on to say— "that she has been regularly patented, it follows that the ownership of the patent, including the child herself, belongs to you, and will pass at your death into the possession of your heirs. Holding the patent, they can prevent any husband taking possession of the girl by marriage, and they can sell, assign, transfer, and set over the patent-right and the accompanying girl to any purchaser. If she is sold to a speculator or to a joint stock company, she will find her position a most unpleasant one. To sum up the case, madam, either your child is patented or she is not. If she is not patented, you are guilty of forgery. If she is patented, she is an object of barter and sale, or, in other words, a chattel."

This was certainly a wretched state of things, and Mrs. Smith, to ease her mind, began to abuse Mrs. Brown, whose stove had branded the unfortunate little girl. She loudly insisted that the whole fault rested with Mrs. Brown, and demanded to know if the latter could not be punished. The young man, who was immensely learned in the law, thereupon began a new argument. He told her that where there is a wrong there must, in the nature of things, be a remedy. "Mrs. Brown, by means of her stove, has done you a great wrong. In accordance with the maxim, '*qui facit per alium facit per se,* Mrs. Brown, and not the stove, is the party from whom you must demand redress. She has wickedly and maliciously, and at the instigation of the devil, branded your child, and thus rendered you liable for an infringement of the patent law. It is my opinion, madam, that an action for assault and an action for libel will both lie against Mrs. Brown, and, '*semble,*' that there is

also ground for having her indicted for procure-
ment of forgery." Finally, after much further
argument, the young man advised her to apply to
a magistrate and procure the arrest and punishment of Mrs. Brown. ·

Accordingly, Mrs. Smith applied to the Mayor,
who, after vainly trying to comprehend the case
and to find out what was the precise crime alleged
against Mrs. Brown, compromised the matter by
unofficially asking that lady to appear before him.
When both the ladies were in court, Mrs. Smith,
prompted by the clerk, put her complaint in the
shape of a charge that Mrs. Brown had branded
the youthful Smith girl. The latter was then
marked " Exhibit A," and formally put in evidence,
and both complainant and defendant told their respective stories.

The result was that the court, in a very able
and voluminous opinion, decided that nobody was
guilty of anything, but that, with a view of avoid-
ing the penalty of infringing the patent law, the
mother must apply to Congress for a special act

declaring the child regularly and legally patented. If Congress finds time to attend ·to this important matter, little Miss Smith will be the first girl ever patented in this country, and the legal profession will watch with unflagging ·interest the lawsuits to which in future any infringement of the patent may lead.

RIGHTEOUS RETRIBUTION.

MRS. Col. Lewis, of Clinton, Ill., is universally respected by those who know her. It is certainly not her fault that she was constructed at a period when the "sugar and spice, and everything nice," which Dr. WATTS assures us are the chief ingredients of girls, were apparently exhausted, and there were no materials available except vinegar and mustard. In spite of her severe and acrid disposition, no one doubts that she is a sincere and earnest woman. She has a soul above frivolity and pleasure, and she is unsparing in her denunciations of the wicked. Of course, she is not the sort of woman with whom one would care to take long walks in the country, but her boldness and inflexible adherence to the path of duty compel public respect.

To this good woman her husband is a constant

trial. Col. Lewis is a man of excellent moral character and sandy hair, but he has an undeniable fondness for innocent flirtation, which, in his wife's estimation, is the gravest of all crimes. Naturally, she throws all possible obstacles in her husband's objectionable path. But the world is full of girls and, except when the Colonel is locked up in his bedroom by his determined wife, she can never be absolutely sure that he is not wrecking her domestic happiness by bowing to young ladies, or by saying good morning to wicked married women who have the audacity to be beautiful, and who aggravate that crime by assuming a pleasant and genial manner.

Three weeks ago Clinton resolved to have its first masked ball. It is needless to say that Mrs. Lewis was shocked when she learned that this infamous scheme was advocated by several hitherto respectable people, and that it was reasonably certain to be successfully carried out. To her delight, Col. Lewis expressed to her his strong disapprobation of masked balls, and said that he was really glad that business interests would require his presence in Chicago on the night of the contemplated crime. A week before that date, however, she was horrified at discovering in the Colonel's desk a catalogue of fancy costumes which a Chicago tradesman offered to let upon very reasonable terms to persons about to attend masked balls. Among these costumes was one which was designed to enable the wearer to personate a horse. It consisted chiefly of a horse's head and silk tights. An unfinished letter in the handwriting of the Colonel showed that the wretched man intended to be present at the masquerade in this revolting costume, and that his pretence of business at Chicago was merely designed to deceive the wife of his bosom. It was a crushing blow, but that intrepid woman bore it nobly. Instead of acquainting Col. Lewis with her knowledge of his guilt, Mrs. Lewis instantly wrote to the costumer, ordering the dress of a jockey to be sent to her. When, twelve hours before the evening of the ball, her husband bade her good-bye and ostensibly started for Chicago, she never intimated that she knew his plans, but she took leave of him almost tenderly. That misguided man went no further than the next street, where he concealed himself in the house of a depraved friend, and chuckled over the way in which he " had sold the old woman."

It was not until ten o'clock in the evening that Col. Lewis, beautifully arrayed in his equine costume, and exhibiting the faultless proportions of his manly legs, entered the ball-room. The beauty and fashion of Clinton were already assembled, and among them was a closely-masked lady wearing the dress of a horse-jockey and carrying a riding-whip. No one dreamed that she was the severe and earnest Mrs. Lewis, for a lavish use of the great staple of the Gulf States had wrought so marvelous a change in her dimensions that her husband mistook her for a blooming corn-fed beauty of Peoria. In fact she was the very first lady to whom he addressed himself, and when his first compliment was answered by a blow of the whip on his unprotected legs, he almost doubted whether he would not follow her even at the risk of a second blow.

Prudence, however, prevailed, and the gallant Colonel selected another lady as the object of his attentions. He was just beginning a promising flirtation when the avenging jockey smote his calves, and in a thoroughly professional tone ordered him to "g'lang now." His tights were very thin, and the blow wrung from him a hasty theological expression, which caused the object of his attentions to hurriedly leave him. Meanwhile, the cruel jockey had passed on and vanished in the crowd, and it was several minutes before Col. Lewis could bring himself to cease rubbing his suffering legs, and to resume the attempt to enjoy the ball. When next he accosted a fair masker, he looked anxiously around for the jockey, and not perceiving her, took courage and began a new flirtation. He was just about to request the honor of a waltz when two swift and cruel blows descended upon his already lacerated extremities, and the

voice of the terrible jockey counseled him to
" g'lang," and likewise to " gettup."   The miserable man forgot his partner, and limping to a seat,
sat down and indulged in language which, had he
not spoken in a suppressed tone, would have cast
a sulphurous glare over the assembly.

Twice more during the evening did the wretched
Colonel try to mingle in the gayeties of the ball,
but each time the awful jockey, inexorable as fate,
lashed him with constantly increasing violence.
When he was about to enter the supper room she
followed him closely, and so emphasized her suggestion that he should descend to the stable in
search of oats, that in mingled despair and rage he
fled from the ball-room to return no more.   The
jockey lingered until the ball was over, and then,
full of peace and triumphant joy, sought her home.

For once Mrs. Lewis, although she was a woman,
was magnanimous.   When her unhappy husband
returned from his pretended trip to Chicago, she
never once mentioned the ball to him, but quietly
handing him her jockey costume, told him to send

it to the owner and pay the bill, adding that he
would find a bottle of arnica in his room. The
cotton was, it is believed, subsequently used in the
manufacture of two "comfortables" of extra thick-
ness, and the Colonel presented his wife with a new
silk dress, a set of furs, and a costly bracelet. It
is thought that he will never attend another
masked ball, and that he will shoot any man who
mentions the subject in his hearing.

PRACTICE AMONG THE PIUTES.

THE Piutes are not among the most intelligent or warlike of our Indian tribes. Indeed, they are generally treated with contempt by the bold miners of the Pacific slope, who speak of them much in the same tone as that used by a practical statesman when discussing the question of civil service reform with the frequenters of his bar-room. Still, the Piutes are by no means stupid. If a solitary and unarmed white man, with a good head of hair, comes within a Piute's reach, he knows what to do with that hair quite as well as if he were a Sioux or an Apache. Similarly, he fully comprehends the uses of whisky, and there are said to be occasional Piutes who have mastered the profound principles of draw-poker. When it is also mentioned that the Piutes have thrown open the profession of medicine to women, with a hearty

PRACTICE AMONG THE PIUTES.

liberality as yet unknown among whiter and more civilized people, the fair sex can hardly fail to conceive a warm regard for that peaceful and progressive tribe.

There are certain features connected with the practice of medicine among the Piutes by female physicians which show that the whole community takes a warm interest in the matter. In England and among the white people of this country the female doctor can hope for nothing more than cold toleration. No venerable male physician, for example, pats Dr. MARY WALKER on the shoulder, and smilingly remarks, " Go on, dear little girl, in your noble career, and may your drugs prove half as efficacious as your beautiful smile and the soft rustle of your coat-tails." If our female doctors happen to cure a patient, the cold world ignores their skill and insinuates that nature alone deserves the credit of the cure ; while if the patient dies no one pays the female doctor the common courtesy of suggesting that she is in partnership with the undertaker. The general attitude of the public toward female physicians is that of affected disbelief in their ability either to kill or to cure, and of entire indifference as to the actual results—if any —of their practice. How differently this matter is viewed by the Piutes will appear from the following incident in the career of a Piute medicine woman.

The medicine woman in question wore the simple, modest, yet picturesque name of "Heap-Chokee," a name given to her in memory of the able manner in which, during her fifteenth year, she strangled two wounded emigrants whom her dear father had previously scalped. She became a widow at the age of sixty, and having been duly examined by the chief men of the tribe and pronounced to be far too ugly for matrimonial purposes, she was duly licensed to practice medicine according to the tenets of the regular Piute medical school.

Shortly afterward Dr. Heap-Chokee was called in to prescribe for a squaw who was in the last stages of consumption. Having made a careful ex-

amination of the patient by punching her in tender
places with the handle of a hoe, the doctor decided
that the case was one which did not call for drugs,
but for " pow-wow." She therefore shut herself
up in the patient's wigwam, and danced and howled
with much vigor for several hours, at the expira-
tion of which the patient was found to be dead.
It so happened that the consumptive squaw was
not a valuable one, and, in fact, her husband was
rather glad that she was dead. Still, the death of
the doctor's first patient was not adapted to give
her a reputation for medical skill, and the affair
was therefore investigated by a council of able
warriors. The council decided 'that the doctor
had committed an error in not prescribing medicine,
and while it was expressly conceded that it was
not worth while to severely reprimand her for the
death of a valueless squaw, she was affectionately
warned that she would do well in future to prescribe a good dose of real medicine.

A fortnight later a young warrior was brought
into camp suffering from an acute attack of grizzly

bear, the leading symptoms of which were the fracture of a dozen or two of his ribs and a general mashing of the internal organs. This time the doctor compounded a medicine that really ought to have worked wonders. It was made by boiling together a collection of miscellaneous weeds, a handful of chewing tobacco, the heads of four rattlesnakes, and a select assortment of worn-out moccasins. The decoction thus obtained was seasoned with a little crude petroleum and a large quantity of red pepper, and the patient was directed to take a pint of the mixture every half hour. He was a brave man, conspicuous for his fortitude under suffering, but after taking his first dose, he turned over and died with the utmost expedition.

Again the council of leading warriors investigated the case. They analyzed and tasted the medicine, and agreed that it was faultless in its way, and strong enough to cure any reasonable disease. While they fully approved of the prescription, they found that the doctor had relied upon it alone, and had omitted to dance and yell to any extent worth mentioning. This innovation upon the recognized method of treating diseases could not be passed over in silence, and Dr. Heap-Chokee was solemnly warned that she must either practice medicine properly or meet the consequences, and that young and valuable warriors could not be wasted with impunity.

Soon after the daughter of the leading chief was attacked by what was undoubtedly an inflammation of the brain. Warned by experience, the doctor brought the entire resources of the medical art to bear upon the case. She not only administered large doses of her favorite decoction, but she took a large tin pan into the patient's wigwam and hammered it for twenty-four hours, during which time she never ceased to dance and to yell at the top of her lungs. Her zeal called forth the admiration of the whole tribe, and it was considered certain that the patient must recover, but, strange as it may seem, the doctor emerged from the wigwam in the morning of the second day and sadly announced that the girl was dead.

Once more the council met, but its deliberations were short. Dr. Heap-Chokee had attended three patients and every one had died. There could be no doubt that she was an unsuccessful physician, and that if she continued to practice the tribe would soon become extinct. The course to be pursued was too plain to be ignored. The doctor was summoned, and was mildly but firmly told that her professional career was at an end. Three warriors then led her outside the limits of the camp, and administered to her six revolver-bullets, after which lots were drawn for the possession of her scalp, and the rest of her was quietly buried.

The Piutes may be dull and ignorant savages in comparison with ourselves, but it is a false pride which would forbid us to learn from them any really useful lesson. The warm interest which they take in the success of female physicians is conspicuously at variance with the indifference which we exhibit, and there is certainly something in the example which they set us that we might do well to follow.

GIBBERISH.

IT is estimated that there are at this moment seven million small boys in this country. Of this number—if we except those who are deaf, dumb, blind, and idiotic—there is not one who is not familiar with that mystic formula known as "aina maina mona mike," and who does not habitually use it as a means of divining who shall be "it," in the various games incident to boyhood. How each successive generation of small-boys comes into the possession of this formula is one of the most profound and difficult questions of the age.

The superficial thinker fancies that the solution of this problem is a very simple one. He hastily assumes that one generation teaches "aina maina" to its successors, and that the knowledge of the formula is thus handed down from father to son. But is there a single instance on record in which a father has deliberately imparted this knowledge to his son? We all know from our own experience that long before we have arrived at manhood, and become seized and possessed of our personal small-boy, we have forgotten the lore of our childhood, and, hence, are not in a condition to impart it to any one. There always comes a period in our lives when we hear our sons rehearsing "aina maina" with confidence and accuracy, and as we suddenly remember that we, too, once knew those mystic words, we wonder from whence the new generation of small-boys learned them. The fact that fathers do not teach them to their sons will appear so plain, upon a very little reflection, that it is unnecessary to dwell longer upon it at this time. In whatever way the venerable formula comes into the possession of one generation, it is quite certain that it is not learned from the previous generation.

It is a noteworthy fact that no small-boy is ever able to tell from whom he learned "aina maina." If we ask any casual small-boy who taught him the mysterious syllables, he will invariably reply "Dunno," and promptly change the subject. We cannot tell how we ourselves learned them, and all our memory can tell us is that there was an exceedingly remote period when we did not know them, and a somewhat later period when they were perfectly familiar to us. Here then we have the remarkable phenomenon of an elaborate formula in an unknown tongue, which every boy knows, without knowing from what source he learned it, and as to which we simply know that he does not learn it from the preceding generation. Whence comes this knowledge, and in what way is it handed down through the centuries? This is a problem which Sir Isaac Newton said he "would be hanged if he could solve," and of which Comte remarked "that it is beyond the limit of our intellectual powers, and hence should not receive the slightest attention."

The ancient sages and philosophers were as much in the dark as to this matter as we are.

PLATO mentions that IPHIGENIA was selected for the
sacrifice by a soothsayer, who repeated "aina
maina" until the lot fell upon that unhappy
damsel; and he adds, "that this method of divina-
tion was brought to Greece by CADMUS, who doubtless learned it from the barbarians." This may or
may not be true, but in either case it throws no
light upon the question how the formula has been
handed down to the present day. SOCRATES alluded to the matter once, if not twice, and is reported to have said to ALCIBIADES: " Tell me now,
ALCIBIADES, whence did you learn to divine through
(or by means of) ' aina maina '?" to which ALCIB-
IADES replied, "I dunno." " Then," continued the
sage, " it is impious for you to ask me how it happened that I was last night banged as to the head
with the dirt-devouring broom; for he has no right
to propose delicate personal conundrums who is
unable, whether through his own dullness or the
displeasure of the gods, to answer simple and easy
questions in two syllables." This conversation
shows that SOCRATES perceived the mystery which

enshrouds the subject, but it does not appear that he ever successfully penetrated it.

Now, it is evident that if the knowledge of this strange formula is not taught by one generation to another—and we know perfectly well that it is not —it must be developed spontaneously in every small-boy's mind. The small-boy has his measles and chicken-pox, and other strictly juvenile physical diseases, and he ought, by analogy, to have some form of mental disease peculiar to his age. Medical men are well aware that talking in unknown tongues—or gibbering, as it is usually called—is a symptom of certain forms of brain disease, and it is credibly asserted that most of the remarks made in unknown tongues by the followers of the erratic EDWARD IRVING, were simply repetitions of " aina maina." Let us, then, suppose that when the small-boy suddenly breaks out with the same curious formula, it is a symptom of a juvenile brain disease, just as the eruption which at some time roughens every small-boy's surface is a symptom of chicken-pox. This hypothesis fully explains the whole mystery. No small-boy learns the chicken-pox from his father, and yet every small-boy has it. No small-boy learns "aina maina" from his father, and yet if a small-boy were to be kept in solitary confinement from his birth up to his fourteenth year, he would infallibly break out with the knowledge of "aina maina." When a hypothesis meets all the facts of any given case, it may properly be accepted until another and better hypothesis is devised. The hypothesis that this knowledge of "aina maina" is a symptom of brain disease, stands precisely upon the same ground as the hypothesis of development, and the moment this fact is brought to Professor HUXLEY's attention he will adopt the one as eagerly as he has adopted the other.

CARRIE'S COMEDY.

DR. BARTHOLOMEW, of Towanda Falls, Pennsylvania, is the proud possessor of an extremely precocious child. Miss CARRIE BARTHOLOMEW is only ten years old, but, nevertheless, she is a young person of extraordinary acquirements and conspicuous culture. At the age of six she could read with great ease, and before reaching her eighth birthday she had developed a marked taste for novel-reading. About the same period she made her first attempt at authorship, and soon achieved an enviable reputation in several local nurseries, where her fairy tales were recited with immense applause. In her ninth year she wrote a novel, of which, unfortunately, no copies are now in existence, and began an epic in six books upon " St. Bartholomew's Day "—which sanguinary event she classed among the ancestors of her family. The

epic was discontinued after the completion of the
second book, owing to the premature extermination
of the Huguenots, but the young author lashed the
Catholic party with great vigor, and denounced
CHARLES IX. as the scarlet person mentioned in
the Apocalypse. The latest effort of Miss BAR-
THOLOMEW was, in all respects, her crowning work.
It was a drama in blank verse and in five acts,
entitled "Robinson Crusoe; or, the Exile of
Twenty Years," and it was publicly performed in
the Baptist lecture-room by a company of children
drilled by the author. The proceeds of the entertainment were designed for the conversion of the
heathen, and it was attended by a large and hila-
rious audience.

The entire work of mounting the drama fell
upon the shoulders of the author. The stage was
beautifully ornamented with borrowed shawls; and
three fire-screens, covered with wall-paper and with
tree and flower patterns, did duty as scenery.
The costumes were unique and beautiful, and a
piano ably played by a grown-up young lady sup-

plied the place of an orchestra. The curtain rose at the appointed time, and displayed *Crusoe* in his English home in the act of taking tea with his wife. A cradle in the corner held a young Crusoe— played with much dignity by Miss BARTHOLOMEW'S best doll—and a wooden dog reposed on the hearth- rug. *Crusoe*, after finding fault with the amount of sugar in his tea—a touch that was recognized as wonderfully true to life—announced that he was to sail the next morning on a voyage to South Amer- ica. *Mrs. Crusoe* instantly burst into tears, and remarked :

"Our wedded life has scarce begun !
But three months since you led me to the altar,
And now you leave me, friendless and forlorn !"

Crusoe, however, soon comforted his wife, and bidding her teach her surprisingly precipitate in- fant to revere his absent father, put on his ulster, and after a last passionate embrace, departed for South America.

The second act presented *Crusoe* in his island home, clad chiefly in seal-skin jackets, and much given to pacing the ground and soliloquizing. According to his account, he had now been on the island three years, and was beginning to feel rather lonesome. He referred in the most affectionate terms to the sole comrade of his joys and sorrows, his gentle goat—which animal, hired for the occasion, from a Towanda Falls Irishman, was conspicuously tethered in the background, and would obviously have butted *Crusoe* into remote futurity if he could have broken loose. Presently *Crusoe* heard a faint yell in the distance, and decided that it was made by a cannibal picnic party, whereupon he announced that he would go for his gun and sweep the wicked cannibals into the Gulf.

Act three was brought to an unexpected but effective climax. It opened with the entrance of a dozen assorted cannibals dragging two helpless prisoners, who were securely bound. After an effective war-dance, one of the prisoners was killed with a club, and was placed on a painted fire. Just as the chief cannibal had announced that the dinner was nearly cooked, *Crusoe's* goat, which had managed to escape from the green-room, burst upon the cannibals. Two of them were knocked over into the audience, where they wept bitterly; others were strewn over the stage, while a remnant escaped behind the scenes. The prisoner, in spite of the fact that he was dead and roasted, fled at the first onset of the goat, and the curtain was dropped amid wild applause. After the goat had been captured by some male members of the audience, and *Crusoe* himself had explained that his proposed massacre of the cannibals had been unintentionally anticipated, the stage was set for the fourth act, and the play went on.

This particular act was a magnificent proof of the author's originality. The rising of the curtain displayed *Crusoe* sitting on a grassy bank, surrounded by four children, whom he calmly alleged to be his own. Beyond vaguely alluding to them as the gift of heaven sent to cheer his lonely hours, that astonishing father did not offer to account for their origin. The author's chief object in introducing them was, however, soon disclosed. *Friday*, who presently appeared, and whose lack of any ostensible origin was doubtless due to the recent interference of the goat, was requested to sit down and undergo instruction in the Westminster Catechism. The scene that followed was closely modeled after the exercises of an ordinary Sunday-school; and *Crusoe's* four inexplicable children sang songs to an extent that clearly proved that singing was the object of their remarkable creation. Lest this scene should appear somewhat too solemn, the author judiciously lightened it by the happy expedient of making *Friday* a negro, who constantly said "Yes! Massa," and " yah yah!" and who always spoke of himself as "dis child." Altogether, the act was a delightful one, and whenever *Crusoe* alluded to his "dear children," and regretted that they had never seen their dear mamma, the audience howled with rapture.

How *Crusoe* and his interesting family escaped from the island the author omitted to mention.

The fifth and last act depicted his arrival home and his final reunion with the bride of his youth. *Mrs. Crusoe* was sitting at her original tea-table, precisely as she was in the habit of doing twenty years earlier, when there was a knock at the door, and *Crusoe* entered, followed by his four children and *Friday* carrying a large carpet-bag and a bundle of shawls. Mutually exclaiming " 'Tis he," and " 'Tis she," the long-separated husband and wife rushed into each other's arms. After the first greetings were over, *Crusoe* remarking in the most elegant blank verse that though he had brought neither gold nor gems, he had nevertheless returned rich, presented in evidence thereof his four children. Whereupon that noble woman, remarking that she, too, had been wonderfully blest, brought in seven children from the next room and told them to kiss their father. After which the drama was brought to a graceful end by the singing of "Home, Sweet Home," by the entire strength of the Crusoe family.

For originality and rare dramatic genius, it is

clear that this play has never been equaled by any previous American dramatist; and we may be sure Miss CARRIE BARTHOLOMEW will in future look back upon it with at least as much wonder as pride.

A CHICAGO IDYL.

A GREAT intellect can be confined in a small body, but a large foot cannot be comfortably compressed into a small shoe. Mr. STANLEY MATTHEWS, for example, who is believed to have at least twenty-seven more cubic feet of intellect than any other man now living, is able to successfully conceal the whole of it in one or another part of his body, but he would be utterly unable to crowd one of his feet into Mrs. MATTHEWS' slipper. Nevertheless, man is so constituted as to be a constant prey to the belief that he can wear shoes several sizes too small for him, from whence arise physical agony, vexation of spirit, and grievous violations of the third commandment.

It is rare that a young man is as modest and bashful as is a certain young man now residing in Chicago. He is an excellent youth, but it has

been frequently asserted by his female acquaintances that should he ever be placed in circumstances
where it would be his duty to remark " boo " to a
goose, he would fail to make that remark. His
present occupation is the study of chemistry, and
he has blown himself up so many times that the
small stock of self-confidence which he may originally have had has completely vanished. Nevertheless, he had the strange audacity to fall violently
in love with a beautiful young lady, the daughter
of a grim and prosaic Chicago pork person, and
continued to prosecute his suit in spite of the
brutal want of respect shown to him by the father,
who would frequently call down over the banisters
to his daughter, in whose society the bashful young
man was lingering—" Jane! it's eleven o'clock.
Turn out that there gas and come to bed this
minute."

Not very long ago there was a concert at the
Chicago opera-house, to which the bashful lover
escorted the object of his affections. It was the
first time that he had ever visited a public place in

company with a lady, and he was naturally extremely nervous. He dressed himself with the greatest care, and put on a new pair of patent leather gaiters purchased expressly for the occasion. Of course, the gaiters were much too small for him, for, as Sir ISAAC NEWTON conclusively shows, the size of a lover's shoes varies inversely as the force of his passion. It took him a long while to get into his gaiters, but he accomplished the feat after tremendous efforts, and in due time found himself seated in the parquet of the opera-house, with the beautiful young lady by his side.

There was one of his shoes in particular which inflicted upon him absolutely fiendish tortures, and the latter increased in intensity as the moments came and went. Before the first half of the performance was ended he was nearly wild with pain. It was perfectly obvious to him that either he must obtain immediate relief or become a demonstrative idiot on the spot ; and he therefore availed himself of the screen afforded by the lady's skirts to remove the offending shoe and give liberty to

the captive foot. It was his intention to put the
gaiter on again, at the close of the concert, without
attracting attention, and had it not been for an un-
foreseen accident his purpose might have been
carried into effect.

It so happened that he occupied a seat next to
the aisle. Soon after he had removed the shoe, a
lady who sat on the same row of seats rose up to
leave the house. As she brushed by the bashful
young man his disengaged shoe became entangled
under her skirts and was swept away. Half way
up the aisle it escaped from confinement, and became an object of intense interest to several
thoughtless young men, one of whom finally seized
it and tossed it in a playful Chicago fashion into
the lowest gallery.

The full horror of his situation smote the shoe-
less youth. His face became first scarlet and then
pale as he thought of the spectacle he would present when the time should come for him to limp
out of the theatre, with one shoe off and one shoe
on, in little better plight than was the allegori-

cal Richard Doubt mentioned in BUNYAN's *Pilgrim's Progress*. There was no possible lie which he could frame to account for the absence of that shoe, and he knew that his beloved companion would accuse him either of intoxication, of idiocy, or of a penuriousness which permitted him to buy only one shoe at a time. In his great distress, he even attempted to possess himself of one of a pair of India-rubber overshoes which a man sitting in front of him had deposited within reach of his cane, but as he was in the act of drawing the overshoe to him with the handle of his cane he was detected and scowled at with such violence that he was glad to abandon the effort and to murmur an incoherent apology. All this time he kept his unshod foot concealed under the hem of his companion's dress, but he well knew that the hour was rapidly approaching when concealment would be no longer possible. The idea of raising a false alarm of fire, and of imputing the loss of his shoe to the panic which would inevitably ensue, occurred to him ; but his better feelings prevailed, and he resigned himself to his fate. A few days afterward he remembered how he had wished that his lady love was a St. Louis girl, in which case he would have told her all, in the expectation that she would nobly say: "Never mind. Share one of my shoes with me, for it is large enough for us both;" but perhaps the Chicago press is mistaken in its description of the shoes of the girls of St. Louis, in spite of the attention which it has paid to the subject, and perhaps the average St. Louis female shoe is not of abnormal size.

The concert came to an end. With the calmness of desperation the unhappy youth escorted his companion to her carriage amid the sneers and laughter of the heartless public. As he left her at her door, she freezingly remarked that he would never have another opportunity to insult her, and that her father would take prompt measures to punish his outrageous conduct. It is believed that the young man is still alive, and that he has concealed himself in his laboratory. The St. Louis papers, however, think that if he is not dead he ought to be, and that his failure to borrow the young lady's glove and to use it as a temporary substitute for his shoe, no matter how loosely it might have fitted, stamps him as a person devoid of all intelligence and ingenuity.

SCIENTIFIC MENDACITY.

THE dog is a noble animal. No one who has kept a dog in his cellar and noticed the way in which the intelligent beast lays hold of the man who comes to inspect the gas-meter, can help loving and admiring him. Of course, the more we can improve the dog physically, mentally, and morally, the better, and hence every effort at developing new and improved breeds of dogs ought to be warmly welcomed.

Scientific persons also, as well as dogs, deserve, as a general rule, our respect and admiration. Science, if indulged in moderately by men who have strength of mind enough to avoid all mathematical excesses, is a useful and pleasing thing. Every honest and fair-minded man prefers to put confidence in scientific persons, rather than to view them with doubt and suspicion. Nevertheless, it is undeniable that at times certain scientific persons will make assertions which are utterly incredible. Such, it is sad to say, is the conduct of the Scientific Person who, in a recent number of the *Scientific American,* has described a new breed of dog, which he calls "an improved saw-mill dog." The ordinary saw-mill dog, although of mixed and indefinite breed, is a useful animal, and can be trained to catch small pieces of timber that go adrift, as well as to warn children away from the buzz-saw. An improved saw-mill dog would, undoubtedly, be very acceptable, but the alleged animal described by the Scientific Person in question is not merely unprofitable, but is so thoroughly impossible as to be an affront to human intelligence. It is a public duty to expose the mendacious character of this description, and to convict the writer of the unparalleled impudence of which he has ventured to be guilty.

He begins, with a certain degree of moderation, by informing us that the "improved saw-mill dog" is constructed of "the best material, is strong and durable, has very few joints, and retains the log with great firmness." While we do not at once perceive what is gained by diminishing the number of joints with which nature originally provided dogs, there is nothing in the statement just quoted which is absolutely incredible. The writer, however, soon yields to the temptation to play upon public credulity, and informs us that the dog's teeth " are easily taken out and sharpened, or replaced by duplicates! " Is this credible? Who ever heard of taking out a dog's teeth, sharpening them, and returning them to their sockets; or of putting artificial teeth in a dog's mouth? Even were such a thing possible, it would be an atrocious act of cruelty. The Scientific Fabulist, however, is quite willing to be thought guilty of cruelty to animals. He proceeds to say that "shafts"—meaning, of course, clubs—are " convenient and effective in forcing the dogs on to the log and holding them with a relentless grip." That is to say, the poor animals are to be beaten until they bite so deeply in the log which they are required to hold that they may be said to be " forced into it." We don't believe a word of this, for mendacious as the Scientific Person is, he cannot be as cruel as he pretends to be.

He next proceeds to tell us that the dog is " made to slide on an upright bar." This is mere nonsense. A dog might be trained to slide on a nearly horizontal bar, but to make him slide on an upright bar would be impossible. What does this man mean by his preposterous stories? Does he suppose that we are all as ignorant as Western statesmen, or as credulous as Communists? He pretends that the dog's " lower end is pivoted to the knee, and that the upper end will recede and allow large logs to come back." O ! it is, is it? How would the Scientific Person like to have himself pivoted in a similar way ; and if so pivoted would his upper end recede and allow large logs to come back? Does he expect us to believe that logs are intelligent ; that they will run away when the dog is at large, and will have courage to return when they see that he is securely pivoted? It is positively blood-curdling to read the atrocious falsehoods which this shameless person tries to palm off upon us.

The dog's fore-legs are courteously spoken of as arms. This is unobjectionable, but when intelligent men are told that these arms are "made adjustable by spring pins," and can be lengthened or shortened at pleasure, the desire to go and kill the audacious author of such atrocious stories can hardly be restrained. Think of lengthening or shortening a dog's fore-legs at pleasure, either with spring pins or with early summer needles! This is too much. Of course, this is a free country, and a man has a right to free speech, provided he always expresses the sentiments of the majority; but are our homes to be polluted with pretended scientific statements concerning alleged dogs with adjustable fore-legs? If science has come to this, let Mr. COMSTOCK look to it. The United States mails must not and shall not be used to disseminate monstrous scientific falsehoods, subversive of the very first principles of canine anatomy.

Toward the end of his description the scientific moral monster became incoherent. He alludes without any explanation to a "board dog" who, it appears, is "carried in a socket." This may be madness combined with mendacity, and in all probability it is. Then we are told that "the single dog"—what single dog?—"with straight tooth or bit is easily kept in order and easily operated." Who ever said the contrary? Any dog, whether single or wedded, can be kept in order without the slightest trouble if his owner understands the nature and habits of dogs. The Scientific Person, however, may have alluded to the docility of the single dog in order to contrast him with what he calls "improved yielding spring dogs," for he goes on to say that the latter "catch the under side of the cant and hold its lower edge." This man must die. There is nothing else that will satisfy an outraged public. Who ever heard of "improved yielding spring dogs," and what in the name of zoölogy and saw-mills is "the under side of the cant"? We know what scientific cant is, and that it is as disgusting as religious cant, but how can its under side be seized by spring or fall or winter dogs? If there are any improved yielding spring dogs in existence with a fondness for seizing the under side of things, let them be loosed upon the Scientific Munchausen and kept in operation. Such is the very mildest punishment which should be inflicted upon him.

THE BELLE OF VALLEJO.

THE BELLE OF VALLEJO.

VALLEJO, California, possesses a young lady of extraordinary beauty. She is, moreover, as intelligent and bold as she is beautiful, and in grappling with a sudden emergency she is probably unequaled by any one of her sex. Naturally, she is the admiration of every young man in the town. In fact, she is beyond the reach of rivalry. The other young ladies of Vallejo are perfectly well aware that it is hopeless for them to enter the lists with her. They never expect to receive calls from marriageable young men except on the off nights of the Vallejo belle, and, though they doubtless murmur secretly against this dispensation, they apparently accept it as a law of nature.

For two years the beauty in question, whom we will call Miss Ecks, received the homage of her multitudinous admirers, and took an evident delight

in adding to their number.   So far from selecting
any particular young man for front-gate' or back-
piazza duty, she preferred to entertain one or two
dozen simultaneous admirers in the full blaze of
the brilliantly-lighted front parlor.   It is only fair
to add that she was an earnest young woman, who
despised coquetry and never dreamed of showing
favor to one young man in order to exasperate the
rest.

That so brilliant a girl should have finally
selected a meek young minister on whom to lavish
her affections was certainly a surprise to all who
knew her, and when it was first rumored that she
had made such a selection, Vallejo refused to
believe it.   The minister made his regular nightly
calls upon the object of his affections, but an average quantity of eleven other young men never
failed to be present.   Of course, he could not obtain a single moment of private happiness with his
eleven rivals sitting all round the room, unless he
made his evening call at a preposterously early
hour.   He did try this expedient once or twice,

but the only result was that the eleven admirers at
once followed his example. In these circumstances he began to grow thin with suppressed affection, and the young lady, alarmed at his condition,
made up her mind that something must be done
without delay.

About three weeks ago the young minister
presented himself in his beloved's front parlor at
6:50 P. M., and in the ten minutes that elapsed
before the first of his rivals rang the bell, he
painted the misery of courting by battalions in the
most harrowing terms. Miss Ecks listened to him
with deep sympathy, and promised him that if he
would stay until nine o'clock, the last of the objectionable young men would be so thoroughly dis-
posed of that for the rest of the evening he would
have the field to himself. Full of confidence in the
determination and resources of his betrothed, his
spirits returned, and he was about to express his
gratitude with his lips, as well as his heart, when
the first young man was ushered into the room.

Miss Ecks received her unwelcome guest with

great cordiality, and invited him to sit on a chair the back of which was placed close to a door. The door in question opened outward and upon the top of a flight of stairs leading to the cellar. The latch was old and out of order, and the least pressure would cause it to fly open. In pursuance of a deep-laid plan, Miss Ecks so molded her conversation as to place the visitor at his ease. In a very few moments, he ceased to twist his fingers and writhe his legs, and presently tilted back his chair after the manner of a contented and happy man. No sooner did the back of the chair touch the door than the latter flew open, and the unhappy guest disappeared into the cellar with a tremendous crash. Checking the cry that arose from the astonished clergyman, Miss Ecks quietly reclosed the fatal door, placed a fresh chair in its vicinity, and calmly remarked, " That's one of them."

In five minutes more the second young man entered. Like his predecessor, he seated himself on the appointed chair, tipped back upon its hind-legs, and instantly vanished. " That's two of

them," remarked the imperturbable beauty, as she
closed the door and once more re-set the trap.
From this time until nine o'clock a constant suc-
cession of young men went down those cellar-stairs.
Some of them groaned slightly after reaching the
bottom, but not one returned. It was an unusually good night for young men, and Miss Ecks
caught no less than fourteen between seven and
nine o'clock. As the last one disappeared she
turned to her horrified clergyman and said, "That's
the last of them! Now for business!" but that
mild young man had fainted. His nerves were
unable to bear the strain, and when the moment
of his wished-for monopoly of his betrothed had
arrived he was unable to enjoy it.

Later in the evening he revived sufficiently to
seek a railway station and fly forever from his
remorseless charmer. The inquest that was subsequently held upon the fourteen young men will
long be remembered as a most impressive scene.
Miss Ecks was present with her back hair loose,
and the tears stood in her magnificent eyes as she

testified that she could not imagine what induced
the young men to go down cellar.   The jury without the slightest hesitation found that they had
one and all committed suicide, and the coroner
personally thanked the young lady for her lucid
testimony.   She is now more popular than ever,
and, with the loss of her own accepted lover, has
renewed her former fondness for society, and
nightly entertains all the surviving young men of
Vallejo.

This shows what the magnificent climate of
California can accomplish in the production of girls
when it really tries.

THE SLIPPER REPORT.

THE rapidity with which the Bureau of Statistics does its work is admirable. Within a week after New Year's day, the Bureau was able to publish its annual Clerical Slipper Report, which includes complete returns from nearly every Protestant minister in the United States, of whatever denomination. Were it not that the presentation of slippers is a ceremony not recognized by the Church of Rome, the report would, of course, have included a still greater aggregate of slippers, and the task of preparing it would have been proportionally greater. When it is remembered that the 67,418 ministers mentioned in this report are scattered over an entire continent, and that the slippers of each one of them have been accurately enumerated, an approximate idea of the enormous work done by the bureau can be formed.

The total number of clerical slippers presented during the last holiday season was 887,215. These figures represent single slippers and not pairs, as might be hastily imagined—the bureau having been compelled to take cognizance of single slippers only in consequence of the fact that there is a number of one-legged ministers who are never presented with more than one slipper at a time. Even if we divide the figures given in the report by two, and assume that they represent 443,607 pairs of slippers, and only one solitary single slipper, we may well be startled at the immense proportions to which clerical slipper presentation has arrived. The previous report showed that 717,508 single slippers were presented during the holiday season of 1875–6, or 169,707 less than the number mentioned in the present report. A like increase next year will bring more than a million slippers to the parsonages of our land, and it is probable that the number will fall little, if any, short of 1,200,000.

The number of Protestant ministers among

whom these slippers were divided is 67,418.
This gives an average of about thirteen slippers to
each minister. Of course, there was no such im-
partial distribution. While the one-legged Methodist minister at Grand Rapids, Washington Territory, received a solitary slipper made of birch-bark
by an aboriginal parishioner, the fortunate Bishop
of a New England diocese received 73 pairs. The
latter was the highest number of slippers received
by any one clergyman, though a Methodist Pastor
in Chicago and a Cumberland Presbyterian in
Louisville, who received respectively 71 and 70
pairs, were but little behind. About three-sevenths
of all ministers received two and three pairs each,
thus leaving an enormous quantity to be distributed
among the other four-sevenths. It will not escape
the notice of students of the report that Baptist
ministers receive in proportion fewer slippers than
ministers of other denominations. This, however,
is easily explicable upon the theory that the love
and admiration of their flocks are expressed mainly
in the shape of water-proof boots—which latter

articles cannot, of course, be included among slipper statistics.

A new feature has been added to the report this year, which much increases its interest. This is a classification of the slippers in accordance with their patterns. Thus, there are " ecclesiastical" slippers," or slippers bearing ecclesiastical emblems, such as crosses and open Bibles; " slippers of the affections," upon which hearts, clasped hands, and such like devices are embroidered; and " textual slippers," which are ornamented with the chapter and verse of some particular text; as, for example, "Luke xcviii : 17." Apparently, slippers of this kind are presented chiefly to unmarried ministers, since the majority of them refer to texts inculcating the duty of marriage. " Motto slippers " are evidently extremely popular, for it appears that no less than 2,170 slippers bore the legend " Bless our Pastor." Among " miscellaneous slippers," a pair which were embroidered with a beautiful picture of DANIEL in the Lion's Den is mentioned, and it is to be regretted that the artist, owing to want of space, was compelled to put the lions on one slipper and DANIEL on the other; thus seriously interfering with the unity of the design.

What becomes of all these slippers? It is well known that a popular clergyman never ventures to wear his Christmas slippers, for the reason that whatever pair he may wear, he thereby incurs the anger of the givers of the other pairs. Of course, he cannot openly sell his superfluous slippers, and he cannot give them away or destroy them. It is thus seen that the question " what does he do with them ?" is one that touches a great and solemn mystery. Hitherto no one has been able to solve this mystery, but unless we are grossly deceived, the clue to it is at length in our hands.

It would occur to the dullest mind that the existence of a " Clerical Co-operative Slipper Society and India-rubber Guild " must have some connection with clerical Christmas slippers, but a copy of the constitution and by-laws of the Society, which, in spite of the secrecy in which the matter has hitherto been shrouded, recently came into the

5

hands of a well-known resident of this city, throws a flood of light upon the slipper problem. Under the rules of the Society every member forwards his slippers and India-rubbers to the Central Agency, in Boston. The agency forwards them to London, where they are quietly sold by a sub-agent. From the proceeds are first paid the salaries of the chief agent and his assistants and the cost of handling the slippers. The rest of the money is then divided pro rata among the original slipper-owners, each of whom pledges himself to devote a tenth of his annual receipts to purchasing shoes for barefooted children. The Society recognizes no ecclesiastical or sectarian differences. The Episcopal Bishop and the Primitive Methodist minister are united by the common bond of superfluous slippers. At what rate the slippers are sold and what is the average amount per pair which each member of the Society receives the public will doubtless learn at a later day. All that is now known of the society is its existence and its method of operation. Of these there can be no doubt, provided, of course, the well-known citizen to whom reference has just been made is as trustworthy as he is universally believed to be.

Hitherto Congress has not ordered the Slipper Report to be printed for public distribution, but it is earnestly to be hoped that the present report will be printed, and that every citizen will receive and study a copy of what is really one of the most able documents ever prepared.

POPULAR ELECTRICITY.

WITHIN the present century vast progress has been made in the study of the nature and applications of electricity. From the first sparks drawn from the back of the primeval cat by her cave-dwelling master, to the discovery of the phonograph, there is an immense distance. Nevertheless, it is believed by many scientific persons that we are as yet merely on the threshold of electricity, and that in the future we shall make discoveries infinitely more important than those which the ablest electricians have hitherto made.

It is only just beginning to be understood that the electric currents of the earth have an intimate connection with a great quantity of things. The aurora-borealis is believed to be in some mysterious way connected with spots on the solar disk, and these spots in their turn have an influence upon our climate, and upon the spread of pestilential diseases. Recently it has been asserted that no man can sleep well unless the major axis of his bed, and consequently his personal major axis, corresponds with the position of the axis of the earth. This is due to the fact that the currents of earthly electricity flow in the direction of the earth's axis; or, in other words, from pole to pole. If they enter a recumbent human being at his feet, and pass out at his head, he becomes sleepy, while if, owing to the wrong position of his bed, they enter him from one side or the other, their struggles to get out again produce such a derangement of his nervous system, as to render it impossible for him to sleep. These are but a few of the hosts of facts which might be mentioned to prove the influence of earth-currents upon man and his surroundings, and we shall yet make discoveries in this particular field, which no one outside of an insane asylum will be capable of believing.

The reason why the cats whose howls disturb our nocturnal slumbers are uniformly found on

back fences running in a direction perpendicular, or
nearly perpendicular to the axis of the earth, has
never hitherto been ascertained. Sir ISAAC NEWTON
attempted to explain the fact by asserting that the
great majority of fences are built parallel to the
equator, but this explanation is glaringly at variance
with well-ascertained facts. BUFFON suggested that
cats are mysteriously influenced by the moon, and
that hence they prefer fences which are built in the
general direction of the plane of the moon's orbit.
This is certainly a plausible explanation, but it has
yet to be proved that moonlight is the cause, rather
than a mere incident, of nocturnal cat concerts.
The other explanations which have been hazarded
by lesser authorities are scarcely worth mentioning. All that we really know is the single fact
that nocturnal cats are distributed around the
earth in belts parallel to the equator. Fully
ninety-three per cent of the cats that bring us from
our midnight couches with bootjacks in our hands
and rage in our hearts, are found perched upon
the east and west fences, and to the truth of

this assertion every New Yorker will readily agree.

In examining this very interesting and important problem, let us begin by asking why the midnight cat howls. Superficial observers have alleged that howling is the natural expression of the tender passion among cats, and that the intensity of a cat's admiration for the female of his species may be accurately measured by the hideousness of his howls. This is an insult to human intelligence and feline self-respect. Would any young man, desiring to plead his suit with the lady of his heart, place himself under her window and yell as if he were undergoing the severest torments ? Of course he would not, and equally of course, no intelligent cat would be guilty of a like folly. The yells of the midnight cat bear every sign of being the expression of the keenest suffering, and only the most perverse ingenuity can regard them as the voice of love.

We have thus learned that the cat perched on a back fence perpendicularly to the axis of the earth, and to the direction of the earth currents of electricity, howls because he—or she, as the case may be—is undergoing acute agony. Very possibly cats pass over fences running from north to south quite as frequently as they do over fences running in the direction of the equator, but in the former case they experience no pain, and hence do not attract attention by their outcries. The moment, however, that a cat finds himself on an east and west fence he is racked by internal pains; he tries to relieve his mind by howls and profanity, and he thereby excites the rage of his human audiences. Now, if we ascertain what produces these pains, we shall have found the true answer to the question under discussion. May it not be that electricity is really at the bottom of the whole affair?

The cat, be it remembered, is more addicted to electricity than any other animal, except the electrical eel, and hence is peculiarly susceptible to the influence of the earth currents. So long as the cat walks over fences running from north to south his

axis is coincident with the direction of these currents. They pass smoothly through his spinal
column, and beyond gently stimulating his mind
and tail, they have no perceptible effect upon him.
When, however, he tries to walk on a fence built
parallel to the equator, his private axis becomes
perpendicular to the earth-currents. They penetrate his vitals and they wrench him all to pieces
in their efforts to force their way through him.
Filled with anguish, he stops, clings fiercely to the
fence, and lifts up his voice in frenzied agony. To
some extent the muscles of his legs are paralyzed,
and he is unable to move until the unfeeling boot-
jack comes hurtling through the air and stimulates
him into action. He then springs from the fence ;
his pains vanish, and his voice is silent. Is not
this a complete and scientific explanation of the
question which has so long defied the ablest scientific minds ?

We thus see how beautiful are the reasoning
processes by which true science investigates
abstruse questions. We also see that one of the

most common incidents of every-night life is due to the electricity of the earth. Let us, then, be thankful that we live in a scientific age, and that there are more uses for electricity than any one has yet dreamed of.

LONG ISLAND HUNTING.

MORE than six months have come and gone since the Long Island Hunt was organized. During that time the gallant hunters have chased the wild anise-seed bag at least twice every week. One would suppose that by this time every member of the hunt must have been in at the death, but, strange as it may seem, not a single anise-seed bag has been killed. A matter so serious as this cannot be passed over in silence, and it becomes necessary to inquire why the chase has in every instance proved unsuccessful.

It will not do to say that the hunters have abstained from killing anise-seed bags in order to avoid the premature extirpation of the animal. Although our most learned naturalists were until recently unaware of the existence of the anise-seed bag on Long Island, there can be no doubt that the

animal is abundant in Queens and Suffolk Counties.
In every instance the dogs have struck the scent
without any difficulty. This shows conclusively
that the covers of Long Island are full of anise-
seed bags, and refutes the pretext that the hunters
forbear to kill because they fear that the animal
will be exterminated.

It is, perhaps, hardly worth while to notice the
ludicrous mistake made by certain provincial papers,
that the anise-seed bag is a literal cloth bag, filled
with a supposed substance called anise-seed, and
dragged on the ground by a mounted groom. The
absurdity of this supposition is glaringly apparent.
Is it probable that a dozen or more men would ride
after a pack of hounds in pursuit of a miserable
prosaic bag? Very small boys might agree to
make believe that a bag is a live animal, just as
very little girls sometimes make believe that a
dust-brush wrapped in a towel is a living infant,
but men have outgrown such childish plays. This
preposterous mistake of the rural press is mentioned
here because it may be reiterated by Philadelphian

or Oshkoshian papers in explanation of the failure
to kill. Chasing wild animals may or may not be
an improving occupation, but the supposition that
the Long Island hunters deliberately chase a
" make-believe " animal, does them a gross injustice.

The anise-seed bag is somewhat larger and
fiercer than the fox, but rather smaller than the
wolf. It is of a light brown color, with an enormous mouth and a fierce disposition. Nevertheless, it shuns the sight of man, and lurks in the
depths of the forest, or makes its way across the
country by availing itself of the shelter of ditches
and stone walls. It is much fleeter than the fox,
but a good pack of hounds can always run it down.
The anise-seed bag, in spite of its fierceness when
driven to bay, rarely attacks man except in numbers,
and when suffering from hunger. In the early history of the Plymouth colonists the anise-seed bags
were very numerous and bold. They would gather
at the outskirts of the settlement in packs of several
hundred, and sit on end howling dismally, and
longing to stay their stomachs with even the most

sour and angular pilgrim in all Plymouth. Still, it
does not appear that any of the colonists were actually killed by these animals. True, we read in the
journal of Capt. MILES STANDISH an entry to the
effect that " it is said that Mr. JOHN ALDEN was
last night devoured by anise-seed bags, and that
his vain and fickle widow is in much tribulation.
There are those who think that he hath received
his deserts; " but it subsequently proved that the
rumor was false. BUFFON asserts that the anise-
seed bag will fight desperately when its means of
escape are cut off, and that the hunter frequently
pays for his temerity with his life. This, however,
was written of the larger species which inhabits the
desert of Gobi, and may not be true of the Long
Island variety. The latter may be as dangerous
as local legends claim that it is; but there is no
well-authenticated case of the death of any Long
Islander at the hands, or rather the teeth, of an
anise-seed bag.

Can it be possible that the gallant huntsmen
who have hitherto ridden so unsuccessfully are

really afraid to bring the animal to bay, lest they or their dogs should suffer serious injury? Although this supposition does no credit to their bravery, it cannot be said to be without some foundation. The huntsmen follow the flying anise-seed bag until the hounds are within a short distance of the animal, when the horses are pulled up, the dogs called off, and the panting anise-seed bag allowed to make its escape. The other day the hounds were so nearly successful in running the beast to earth, that a tame fox was let out of a bag expressly to divert their attention, while the anise-seed bag escaped. As the fox insisted upon lying down to sleep, it was necessary to whip him into activity, and even when this was done, he refused to run, and permitted the master of the hunt to kill him with a club. Why should all this trouble have been taken to prevent the hounds and the huntsmen from reaching the flying anise-seed bag, unless it was that the huntsmen feared to risk an encounter with the desperate animal?

This sort of thing cannot go on indefinitely. Man's dominion over the animals is due to their consciousness that he does not fear them. The smallest puppy will attack the largest man if the latter shows any signs of fear. The anise-seed bags will soon arrive at the opinion that the hunters are afraid of them, and will then introduce a pleasing variety into Long Island hunting. We shall witness the novel spectacle of a dozen scarlet-clad horsemen and a pack of dogs with downcast tails flying across the country with a score of anise-seed bags in swift pursuit. The mind shudders to think what the consequences would be should the unfortunate huntsmen be overtaken, but we cannot shut our eyes to the possibility that such a catastrophe may occur.

The huntsmen must make up their minds to let no more anise-seed bags escape. At the end of the next hunt the brush of the dead animal must be taken. If they are afraid to close with the anise-seed bag at bay, let them abandon the sport at once. If they are not afraid, let them show it by bringing home the brush and pads of the next anise-seed bag that is driven from cover. Their reputation is at stake and it rests with themselves to redeem it.

MAN is the only animal that wears short socks. This is not only a more accurate definition than any hitherto devised by scientific persons, but it shows the inferiority of man to all other animals, and ought to have even more effect in humbling our wicked pride than has the famous story of the little girl who was excessively proud of her silk dress until she was told that it was spun, woven, cut out, made up, and trimmed by a loathsome worm.

The great trouble with the short sock is that it will not keep its place. There being nothing whatever to hold it, the force of gravitation necessarily drags it down about the ankle. This causes an amount of misery which is appalling. There is no man who can feel any confidence in his socks. Whether he is walking or sitting, he knows that

MR. SIMPKIN'S DOWNFALL.

his socks are slowly but surely slipping down. Garters being out of the question, since the shortness of the sock does not permit a garter to be placed in a position where it will not slip, there is absolutely no remedy for what we may fairly call the giant evil of the age. Pins and mucilage have both been tried by desperate men, but they have proved useless, and have merely added to the misery of the user. In these circumstances there is nothing left for man to do except to bear the sock in silence, or to boldly cast it aside and adopt the full-grown stocking.

The latter alternative was recently chosen by that eloquent but unfortunate clergyman, Rev. CHARLES SIMPKINS, of Westbridge, Pennsylvania. Previous to the catastrophe which lately overtook him, the Church did not possess a more popular and promising young clergyman. He could repeat the opening exhortation all the way from "Dearly beloved" to "forgiveness for the same," without once pausing for breath, and it has been asserted that he could monotone the entire Apostles' Creed while breathing only three times. As he was un-married, and not yet twenty-seven years old, he was regarded with peculiar reverence by the un-married ladies of his parish, and he received more annual slippers than any other clergyman in the United States.

·Neatness was one of the distinguishing charac-teristics of Mr. SIMPKINS, and there are probably few men who have suffered more keenly from short socks. When walking through the village, he was in continual dread lest his socks should descend into public view, and even while preaching his most eloquent sermons, the perspiration would gather on his brow as he felt that one of his socks was gradually slipping down. This wore upon him to that extent that his massive intellect threatened to totter, and on the morning of the eighty-first Sunday after Trinity he deliberately paused, after remarking " here endeth "—and stooped down to repair damages. That night he resolved that vigorous measures must be taken, and he accord-ingly wrote a confidential letter to his sister's

husband, who resided in this city, and inclosed the
necessary measurements. Shortly afterward he
received, ostensibly from the husband, but really
from the affectionate sister, two dozen pair of Bal-
briggan hose, together with a pair of scarlet elastics
an inch in width, and of precisely the right size.

As soon as Mr. SIMPKINS had learned by repeated experiment how to wear the scarlet appli-
ances, his spirit began to rise. He was no longer
a prey to doubt and despair. His stockings firmly
kept their place, and he felt that he could even
attend a church picnic and climb over a fence without fear of consequences. Accordingly, for the
first time during his residence at Westbridge, he
consented to attend the Sunday-school picnic of
the 21st of October last, and thereby filled with
unutterable delight the souls of all the unmarried
teachers of the church.

Mr. SIMPKINS, being free from care, entered into
the sports of the picnic with great zest, and the
children insisted that he, together with their teachers, should take part in a game of blind-man's buff.

The request was acceded to, and the usual running, laughing, and shrieking followed. It was while Mr. SIMPKINS was fleeing, in company with six excited teachers, from the pursuit of a blindfolded small boy, that he suddenly noticed that one of his elastics had become unclasped and had fallen to the ground. At the same moment it was perceived by the prettiest of the teachers, who made a frantic effort to seize it, but was anticipated by the unhappy clergyman. It was bad enough for him to know that the teacher had discovered his misfortune, but what was his horror and amazement when, with every appearance of anger, she demanded that he should "hand her that" instantly. He was so astonished at her evident desire to make sport of him that he did not deign to answer her, but put the disputed article in his pocket and walked away. Whereupon the teacher burst into tears and informed her confidential friends that Mr. SIMPKINS had had the inconceivable audacity to steal one of her—in fact, her private property.

The scandal spread rapidly and widely, and

grew as rapidly as it spread.   At the end of half
an hour every lady at the picnic had cut the
clergyman in the most marked manner.   Burning
with shame and indignation, he forgot to repair
the deficiencies of his toilet, and went home feeling rather more crestfallen than did the prophet
DANIEL when he found that the lions would not
recognize his existence.   It was not until he was
on the point of seeking a sleepless pillow that he
discovered that both his scarlet elastics were in
their proper place, while the one which he had
picked up at the picnic lay on his table.   The full
horror of his situation flashed upon him.   The
teacher had really dropped a scarlet elastic, and
he had seized it under the impression that it was
his own.

The utter hopelessness of ever making any
satisfactory explanation of the affair was only too
apparent.   Early the next morning Mr. SIMPKINS
fled from Westbridge a ruined man.   The fatal
articles which had caused his downfall he left behind him, and they teach with mute but powerful

eloquence the lesson that we should bear the socks we have, and never dream of flying to stockings, of which we know nothing except by hearsay.

THE SIX-BUTTON PRINCIPLE.

ALTHOUGH the female dress-reformers always demonstrate at their annual conventions that the practice of supporting stockings by what are deliberately termed ligatures insures the moral and physical ruin of the sex, no successful substitute for the denounced article of dress has yet been invented. Certain dress-reformers have, it is true, devised a system of halyards, brails, and down-hauls, which they assert are far superior to the deadly ligature, but the intricacy of all this running rigging, and the difficulty which inexperienced persons find in its management, have prevented it from coming into use. The inexperienced woman when thus rigged is very apt to make mistakes, and to find herself scudding under bare poles, in consequence of having hauled away on the downhaul when she had merely intended to take a small pull at the halyards. Thus, few persons except dress-reformers are rigged with the improved stocking gear, and even these confess that, for the purpose of catching an early morning train, the despised ligature has its manifest advantages.

About two months ago the ladies of three contiguous counties in Pennsylvania were successively visited by a slight, graceful, and unassuming young woman, who announced that she was the agent of a "Women's Dress-Reform Benevolent Association," and that she desired to call their attention to a new invention of immense hygienic value. The new invention consisted of the application of the six-button-glove principle to hosiery. Of course, this is a delicate subject, but, in the interest of reform and public morality, it must be discussed. It is idle for us to ignore the existence of stockings, and it is cowardly to shrink from performing a public duty because it involves an allusion to a delicate topic. Let us, then, go boldly forward and relate the strange conduct of the unassuming young woman, as reported among the police news of a Pennsylvania paper.

While the substitution of buttons for ligatures or running rigging struck the ladies of the three counties as an admirable invention, the amazing cheapness with which the agent of the alleged association offered to sell the improved garments created immense enthusiasm. She said that the only object of the association was to do good, and that it was therefore prepared to sell the best quality of six-buttoned goods at one-half of their original cost. In confirmation of this statement she submitted lithographic copies of letters from President HAYES, Mr. TILDEN, PETER COOPER, STANLEY MATTHEWS, and other eminent statesmen, all of whom asserted that they felt that the introduction of six-buttoned hosiery was the greatest boon which could be conferred upon the women of America, and simultaneously ordered six dozen pairs of assorted sizes to be sent to their respective addresses. In addition to these letters, the agent exhibited a sample of the garment in question, which appeared to be of the very best quality. The opportunity was one which no prudent lady could permit to pass unimproved, and nearly every one to whom the agent applied ordered at least half a dozen pairs, to be paid for upon delivery.

There was, however, one little preliminary which the agent insisted was indispensable, if she was to execute her orders to the satisfaction of her customers. The human mind shrinks from mentioning this preliminary, but it cannot be ignored. If the buttons were to be of any use, they must be so placed in relation to the button-holes that the garment would be neither too tight nor too loose. Hence, when the agent produced a tape-measure and a note-book, her view of the matter was at once conceded to be correct, and the agent's note-book was furnished with the required data. Thus, that unassuming agent went from house to house throughout almost the whole of three counties, cheering the female population with the hope of miraculously cheap and beautiful hosiery, and filled her note-book with statistics. Unfortunately, that otherwise astute agent drank too much whisky at the last town which she visited, and being arrested for disorderly conduct, confessed that she was a man.

When the ladies who had ordered six-button hosiery learned the truth as to the unassuming agent and the fate which had befallen him, they denounced the wretch with great vigor, and were unanimously of the opinion that a combination of wild horses and red-hot pincers could alone do justice to him. To this outburst of indignation succeeded the terrible thought, what had the felonious agent done with his collection of statistics? Naturally, this thought led straight to hysterics, and for the next week the sale of sal volatile in Central Pennsylvania increased to an unprecedented extent.

A deputation of indignant fathers waited upon the inconceivable villain in jail, and demanded the immediate destruction of his note-book. To this request he declined to accede. He admitted that his pretended association did not exist, and that he had no intention of executing the orders which his deceived customers had given him, but he explained that he was an earnest reformer, and that he intended to publish the statistics in question, in order that the medical fraternity might become convinced of the blighting effect of the ordinary ligature. Nothing could shake his determination. He said that he had a great duty to perform, and that much as it pained him to grieve anybody, he must perform that duty. The indignant parents left his cell much cast down in spirits, and after vainly applying to the local court for an injunction forbidding the false agent to publish his statistics, went home and reported their failure to their wives and daughters.

The one question now agitating the public mind in Pennsylvania is whether that wretched felon will really publish his statistics. The contingency is one which cannot be contemplated without a shudder; but at the same time, it is possible that there is more or less merit in the pretended plan of adapting the six-button-glove principle to more esoteric garments, and that the pretended reformer has really solved the problem with which professional dress-reformers have proved themselves incompetent to grapple.

A REMEDY FOR BRASS INSTRUMENTS.

IN order to be a great military commander it is
generally conceded that a certain amount of indifference to human suffering is requisite. GRANT
would never have dealt his terrible blows at the
army of Gen. LEE, had he been constantly filled
with pity for the tattered and battle-worn Con-
federates, and our President could hardly have
achieved his present proud position as the great
conciliator of the age had his heart continued to
bleed for the poor negro as it bled before the elec-
tion. A like callousness of heart is a necessary
characteristic of the man who undertakes to learn
to play upon a musical instrument.

The sum of human agony caused by the early
efforts of players upon stringed, reed, and brass instruments, is incalculable, and it is noticeable that
wherever musical amateurs abound the Universalist

faith makes no progress, and the Calvinistic doctrine, that a place of future torment is a moral
necessity, finds multitudes of believers. Many
learned commentators have discussed the nature of
the insanity under which King SAUL frequently
suffered, but it is odd that no one has perceived
that it was due to the youthful DAVID's persistent
practice upon the harp. We know that on one
occasion, while DAVID was playing an air, which
doubtless closely resembled " Silver Threads
Among the Gold," SAUL, remarking " S'help me
Father ABRAHAM, this is too much," flung a javelin
at the musician and drove him away. Doubtless,
the king was hasty, but let us remember his extreme provocation. As for DAVID, not content with
having already killed the leading Philistine giant,
he went and played the harp to that unhappy
nation, with the view of demoralizing the people so
that he could make an easy conquest of them on
coming to the Israelitish throne.

While the javelin is probably a specific for all
suffering due to accordeons, violins, cornets, and

flutes, it is not a remedy which is available at the
present day. The most successful mode of treatment which has been devised is that which was
recently tried, with admirable results, in the case
of a young man residing in a Twenty-second street
boarding-house, who was addicted to the French
horn ; and it is due to the medical profession that
the history of the case should be briefly given.

The young man in question occupied the
second-story front hall-bedroom. He was apparently a quiet and well-meaning person, but under
a smooth and spotless shirt-bosom he concealed a
heart heedless of human suffering. It would not
have made much difference where he concealed his
heart, for it would have been quite as callous had
he kept it under his waistband, or inside of his boot.
That he preferred to learn the French horn rather
than any other and more common instrument of
torture, does not palliate his offense ; for although
the horn lacks the ear-piercing shrillness of the
cornet, its tone has a wonderfully penetrating
power, and is to the last degree depressing to the

6*

spirits. Unfortunately, he was free from those forms of vice which lead young men to spend their evenings elsewhere than in their rooms and to lie in bed late in the morning. Moreover, he paid his room rent in advance with cold-blooded punctuality. Hence, although he rose up early and sat up late to practice the horn, his landlady could not make up her mind either to request him to leave or to hint to him, by the discreet method of helping him exclusively to cold coffee and bare bones, that his presence in her house was undesirable.

The man who begins to play a wind instrument employs the most of his time in what may be called "sighting shots." For example, when this particular young man desired to sound B flat, it would take him a long while before he could get his elevation and his wind-gauge regulated. He would hit three or four notes above B flat, and three or four notes below it, a score of times before he would finally make a bull's-eye. Even when, after long effort, he succeeded in hitting the desired note, the sound produced would be what is technically called a "blaat," or, in other words, an uncertain, toneless, and most unmusical sound. It is needless to speak of the effect which this sort of thing had upon his fellow-boarders. At the end of two weeks public indignation had grown to that extent that it was seriously proposed to melt the horn and to pour the metal down the throat of the player, as a warning that unless he promptly reformed he would be dealt with severely. It was then that a homeopathic physician residing in the house called a meeting of the aggrieved boarders in order to propose what he believed would prove a radical cure.

After describing with great clearness the painful symptoms which prolonged practice upon the horn develop in the unfortunate and unwilling listeners, and unfolding at much length HAHNEMANN's theory of cure, he asserted that in order to successfully combat the effects of horn-playing, the use of other instruments which produce analogous symptoms was clearly indicated. Hence, he proposed that each boarder should provide himself with a cornet, a violin, an accordeon, a flute, or a drum, and administer these remedies whenever any symptoms of the French horn wer3 manifested. Few of the boarders believed in homeopathy, but they were in that state of mind in which men clutch at any nostrum which promises relief. They therefore resolved to follow the doctor's prescription, and immediately laid in a full supply of the indicated instruments.

The next evening at seven o'clock the familiar gasp of the horn was heard. Instantly it was followed by the screech of the violin, the spasmodic choking of the cornet, the drone of the accordeon, the wail of the flute, and the fierce uproar of the drum. In two minutes a crowd was collected in the street, under the impression that a large orchestra was rehearsing WAGNER's "Meistersinger," and the young man with the French horn was lying on the floor of his room in strong convulsions.

The cure was complete. Early the next morning the French horn player was removed to a lunatic asylum, where he still remains. He is quiet and harmless, but he believes that he is a remnant of the wall of Jericho, which fell down under the assault of the Hebrew trumpets, and constantly insists that Congress should make an appropriation to repair him and mount him with barbette guns. His horn has vanished, no one knows whither, and the inmates of his former boarding-house are contented and happy. We thus see that homeopathic treatment is certain to cure brass instrument players, and we may be reasonably sure that it would prove equally efficacious in cases of violin and accordeon playing.

SNORING.

THERE is a wide popular misapprehension as to the true nature of snoring. It is almost universally regarded as a mere weakness of the flesh, whereas it is really a crime, and should be treated as such. Instead of being an involuntary act, it is a willful and shameless outrage. It is true that the snorer is usually a person who lacks nervous force and whose physical frame not being kept in constant restraint, becomes limp and loose during sleep and thus readily yields to the temptation to snore. The drunkard is likewise a fickle and irresolute person, who is unable to govern his bodily appetites, but we do not accept this as an excuse for drunkenness. It is the duty of every man to abstain from snoring, no matter how strongly he may be tempted. St. Paul remarked that he "kept his body under," or, in other words, that he did not permit himself to snore, and every person should follow his example. As a matter of fact, it is notorious that no self-respecting person is ever guilty of snoring. Women never snore, except in those rare instances where age has dulled their delicacy, and led them to neglect their hair, and to wear slippers several sizes too large for them. Such women occasionally shock their friends by snoring, but youth and beauty never snore. Among men, snoring must be preceded by a loss of self-respect, and an indifference to the feelings of others. Weak men and coarse men may snore, but no great and good man ever mocked the calm midnight with the brawling of a brutal nose.

In these days when men constantly travel in sleeping-cars, some efficacious prescription for the prevention and cure of snoring is eagerly desired. The most popular remedy for the end in question is a liberal dose of soap—the yellow variety being preferable—inserted in the mouth of the snorer. As a rule, the criminal always lies on his back, and keeps his mouth open. If a wedge-shaped piece of soap, of about the size of a piece of cheese, or say a trifle smaller than a piece of chalk, is placed in the snorer's mouth, he will undergo temporary strangulation, and then sit up and make theological remarks. The trouble with this remedy is that it is not lasting in its effects. The snorer who is soaped will in most cases resume his loathsome practice as soon as he falls asleep. Of course, if he be killed, his snoring is permanently cured, but the sickly sentimentality that is so common in our day renders men shamefully loath to kill even the most abandoned snorer. The recent treatment to which a snorer was subjected on board a Union Pacific sleeping-car was certainly effective, and may afford a useful hint to the traveling public, although it will not, perhaps, prove feasible in all circumstances. The train was bound west, and the rear sleeping-car was nearly full. At the usual hour the beds were made, and the travelers climbed into them with comparatively few contusions. Precisely half an hour afterward a man in one of the lower berths began to snore. His was not the brilliant, brassy snore of the New England nose, but the heavy, sonorous, trombone-like snore of the middle-aged German. In range, power, and tone it was unique, and it instantly awoke the entire company—several of the passengers being impressed with the belief that a collision had occurred, and that a hostile locomotive had entered the car. The noise was endured for a time, with the faint hope that the snorer would strangle himself, but as he settled down to a uniform rhythmic snore, that was evidently meant to last all night, it was felt that active measures were imperatively needed.

The porter was found and bribed to shake the snorer, and to explain to him that his conduct was really intolerable. The culprit awoke with a wild start, made a few feeble remarks in German, and then, sinking back to his pillow, recommenced his refrain. In these circumstances it was plain that the only hope lay in keeping him awake for the rest of the night, and a stalwart Texan, nobly offering to sacrifice his own rest for the benefit of the others, was detailed to constantly prod the German with a stick. Even this plan proved a failure. The snorer could not be thoroughly aroused, and the only effect of the constant insertion of the stick in his ribs was to vary the character of his snore, and to render it rather worse than it had been.

By this time the passengers were convinced that mild measures would never do. A vigilance committee of six members was therefore appointed, and the German, who was a small man, was dragged from his bed and placed on the wood-box in the rear of the car. He was now thoroughly awake, and protested with great vehemence against his treatment. A number of shawl-straps were produced, and he was firmly fastened to a staple, and warned that if he indulged in any further language, or ventured to fall asleep again, he would be taken apart with a screw-driver and distributed along the track. Although he was an obstinate man, he did not lack discretion, and so relapsed into silence.

Gradually the vigilance committee yielded to the desire to sleep, and at eleven o'clock the snorer was left in sole charge of the noble Texan. At 11:15 his head sank on his bosom, and he uttered a prolonged snore that jarred the very frame-work of the car. Grimly the Texan produced from his valise a porous plaster, which he firmly applied to the mouth of the unhappy wretch. The snoring ceased; a few convulsive kicks marred the varnish on the side of the wood-box, and all was still. In the morning the corpse was removed into the baggage-car, and the enthusiastic passengers made up a purse of three hundred dollars, which, together with a beautifully engraved copy of laudatory resolutions, was presented to the ingenious Texan.

It thus appears that a porous plaster when applied to the mouth and nose of a snorer will effect a permanent cure. The only objectionable feature of this mode of treatment consists in the difficulty of disposing of the body. In a city like New York, the meddlesome interference of coroners would prove troublesome.   Still, it is something to know that there is a way of silencing the loudest snore, and at the same time doing something like justice to the wretched victim of an atrocious and wholly inexcusable vice.

THE BAFFLED BOY.

ACCORDING to the best scientific authorities the small-boy becomes a boy at the age of sixteen. At that age he ought to put away small-boyish things, and to put on the bashful awkwardness of semi-intelligent boyhood. At all events, he ought to know that his presence is not desired by young men who come to see his sister. We do not expect this amount of intelligence in the small-boy, and it is often necessary to bribe him with candy or to persuade him with clubs before he will consent to treat his sister with common humanity; but the sixteen-year-old boy usually perceives when an area of courting, accompanied with gradually increasing pressure in the region of the waist and marked depression of the parlor gas, is about to set in, and thereupon discreetly, even if sneeringly, withdraws.

Master Henry T. Johnson, of Warrensburg, Illinois, is a boy who has just reached the period of boyhood, and who is remarkably clever in the invention of traps. If you were to ask him to make you any variety of trap, from a rat-trap to a man-trap, he would satisfy your demand with promptness and skill. His father's premises, both in doors and out, are infested with traps, and there is no style of animal inhabiting Warrensburg that has not been caught in one or another of these traps. On one morning, early in January, it is confidently asserted that no less than two cats, a tramp, a small dog, six chickens, and three small-boys were found in Mr. Johnson's yard in the close embrace of a corresponding number of traps. The truth is the boy has real mechanical genius, and it is a great pity that he is totally lacking in modesty and a regard for the rights of others.

Last fall a young man who had met Master Johnson's sister at a picnic and escorted her home, was seized with a great admiration of Master Johnson's traps, and evinced a great fondness for

that ingenious boy's society.   In fact, he engaged
the boy to give him a series of lessons in trap-
making, and seemed to throw his whole soul into
rat-traps.   Gradually this passion began to fade,
and the young man, instead of studying traps in
the back yard, formed the habit of resting himself
—as he called it—in the parlor with Master JOHN-
SON's sister.   The boy, of course, could not consent
to hurt his friend's feelings by abandoning him to
the society of a mere girl, and, therefore, followed
him into the parlor, and monopolized the conversation.   After a time the young man openly abandoned traps, and only visited the house in the
evenings ; but Master JOHNSON, mindful of the laws
of hospitality, always spent the evenings in the
parlor, and more than once apologized to his friend
for the silence and general uselessness of his sister.
His astonishment, when on one eventful evening
the young man, with the full approbation of his
sister, deliberately told him to "get out," and informed him that if he had not sense enough to know
that he was a nuisance, he would try to knock

sense into him with a base-ball club, cannot be expressed in words. Not only did he wonder at the unscientific idea that sense can be imparted with a base-ball club, but he could not comprehend the young man's sudden dislike of his once-courted society. However, he promptly withdrew, and devoted himself to schemes of swift and deadly vengeance.

For the next week Master JOHNSON spent a large part of his time in the parlor with the doors locked, alleging that he was perfecting a new invention, and that his intellect could not work except in quiet and seclusion. Strange as it may appear, he told the truth. He was perfecting a new kind of trap intended for the benefit of the rude young man and of his unnatural sister. The former was accustomed to sit in a large easy-chair and the latter in a small and fragile rocking-chair on the opposite side of the room. To each of these chairs the boy affixed a most ingenious trap, which was concealed underneath the seat, and was so contrived as to be sprung by the weight of any person who might sit in the chair. If the young man, for example, were to sit down in his accustomed chair, he would be instantly clasped around the waist by a pair of iron arms, while two other iron clasps would seize him by the ankles. A like result would follow any attempt of the sister to seat herself in the rocking-chair, and it was Master JOHNSON's intention, after having caught his game, to leave them for an hour or two in close confinement, and to then read them a severe lecture upon their rudeness.

The young man was due on the next Saturday evening, and Master JOHNSON set his new traps at precisely 7:35 P. M. At 8:40 the young man arrived, and Master JOHNSON ostentatiously marched out of the front gate just as the young man rang the front-door bell. An hour passed, and the revengeful boy returned and listened at the parlor-door, expecting to hear low wails of agony. On the contrary, he heard what seemed to him the outward expressions of much contentment on the part of the young man, and he thereupon entered

7

the room full of fear lest his revenge had miscarried.

He found that the trap which he had set for the rude young man had fulfilled its mission, and that he was held in the firm embrace of the iron bands. To his unutterable surprise, his sister was also caught although her particular trap was unsprung and her chair unoccupied. One pair of iron arms clasped both the victims, and one male and one female ankle were held in close confinement. As the astonished boy entered his sister faintly struggled, but soon resigned herself with Christian patience to her bonds, while the shameless young man pleasantly remarked, "Thank you, HARRY! this trap is worth all the others you ever made, and we wouldn't be let out of it for more than six million dollars." Master HARRY listened to these taunting words; listened also to a renewal of the sounds that he had accurately interpreted as evidence of contentment, and then angrily opening the trap and smashing it to pieces, withdrew to weep in solitude over the failure of his revenge.

This shows that wickedness often overreaches
itself, and that to set two distinct traps for one's
sister and her private young man is as useless as
was the superfluous hole which Sir ISAAC NEWTON
cut for the kitten, he having previously cut a larger
one for the cat.

THE town of Carthage, Mo., was lately surprised by the disappearance of two local smallboys, but the pleasure which this disappearance naturally excited was marred by the fact that two small girls also disappeared. The small-boys were thirteen and fourteen years of age respectively, and were thus too old to be kidnapped and too young to be killed in any " difficulty " or affair of honor. Although, of course, Carthage did not want to recover the missing small-boys, the missing girls were considered sufficiently valuable to be sought for with carefulness and dogs. For a whole week the search was fruitless, and had not one of the smallboys weakly confided in another small-boy, who betrayed him, Carthage would still be mourning its missing children. The story of their disappearance has a fine flavor of romance, and will be of interest to all who have felt a youthful yearning for piracy.

CARTHAGINIAN PIRATES.

JAMES and HENRY, the two erratic young Carthaginians, were violently in love with two contemporaneous small girls. They had full reason to know that their love was returned, and they confided to each other their hopes and fears. Up to a certain point the course of their true loves ran smoothly. They met the girls daily at school, and presented them with apples, slate-pencils, and other pledges of affection. They were not, however, permitted to call upon their beloved objects at the respective homes of the latter, under penalty of being hooted at by cold and brutal small-boys, who had never felt the sacred flame, and who held that a small-boy could not play with a girl without a serious loss of dignity. Of course, they yearned for the uninterrupted society of the loved ones, and after much consultation they decided that the easiest way in which to attain this object would be to seize upon their brides, to make their way to the Spanish Main, and to enter upon a career of piracy. At first the question which one should assume command of the proposed piratical schooner was discussed with a warmth that threatened to wreck the entire scheme, but it was finally agreed that the command should be given to JAMES, but that the first prize captured should be placed under the independent command of HENRY, and that he should at the same time be presented with a two-bladed pen-knife and a set of jack-stones.

This important preliminary being arranged, a night was fixed upon for the intended elopement, and half a pound of molasses candy, four apples, and a set of chessmen were laid in by way of supplies. Each small-boy armed himself with a stout stick, and JAMES also carried a pistol, the efficiency of which was somewhat impaired by the absence of ammunition, and the fact that the pistol had no hammer. In the dead of night, or to be precise, at 7:15 in the evening, the two girls stealthily met their lovers by appointment, behind the barn, and after exchanging a few rapturous endearments, started for the Spanish Main. For obvious reasons, they preferrred the short cut through the fields rather than the turnpike, and after two hours of easy marching they reached a solitary haystack four miles from the town, and in close proximity to an orchard. Here they halted for the night, and excavating niches in the hay, made themselves comparatively comfortable. In fact, they would have been very comfortable had not Capt. JAMES thought it necessary to smoke a cigar in order to keep up his reputation as a bold and hardened pirate. The cigar made him dreadfully sick, and his companions were naturally somewhat cast down at the sight of their commander hovering for hours on the very confines of the basin. Of course, there was no actual basin in the camp, but if there had been, the gallant pirate would have hovered over it to a very great extent.

It is sad to be compelled to mention that pitiless nature, instead of smiling on these preposterous little pirates, rained on them for six consecutive days, confining them closely to the friendly haystack. Marching in the rain was not to be thought of, for although the small-boys calculated that they could reach the Spanish Main in two

days, in spite of the weather, they could not ask
their delicate brides, who had neither umbrellas
nor overshoes, to brave the fury of the elements.
In these circumstances provisions soon became
scarce. Apples were abundant, but apples, when
eaten without other food, pall upon the appetite
after two or three days. The energetic Captain
JAMES led a gallant cutting-out expedition on a
neighboring chicken-coop and captured a hen; but
owing to the absence of matches, the hen could
not be cooked. Finally, the Captain secretly returned to town in search of provisions, and revealed
the location of the haystack to a heartless small-
boy who promptly conveyed the information to the
Captain's father. A company of coarse, prosaic
men thereupon captured the entire expedition, and
the two pirates expiated in their respective wood-
sheds their unholy longing for the Spanish Main.
Bereft of their brides, and placed under strict sur-
veillance, they are now undergoing grinding torments, and it is feared that, thwarted in their practical aspirations, they will become reckless, and

grow up to be savings bank presidents or life insurance officers.

What is remarkable is the fact that in spite of a week spent in a damp haystack without any food but apples, not one member of the expedition wanted to go home. Both the girls and their piratical lovers were thoroughly happy, and protested against being dragged back to Carthage. There are few grown people whose ardor would outlast a week of wet and hunger, and the happiness of the pirates and their brides may well be envied by older and wiser lovers.

TOO MUCH CABBAGE.

THE donation party is a shrewd device on the part of thrifty church-goers to compound for their failure to pay their minister a proper salary by giving him a collection of bulky and cheap articles which he does not want. Still, upon the broad principle that something is better than nothing, the impecunious minister clings to the donation party, and cheerfully hopes that the day will come when his parishioners will cease to believe that a full-grown minister and a growing family can subsist exclusively upon beans and pen-wipers. In its inception, the donation party was, of course, a voluntary affair; but in many places it is now as regular and inevitable as Christmas. Occasionally a congregation endeavors to let the season pass by unnoticed, but in most cases the minister boldly meets the emergency by announcing from the pulpit that " the annual visit to the pastor " will take place on such a day ; whereupon the congregation meekly collects its beans and pen-wipers, and testifies in the usual manner its love for its pastor.

The donation party is a very depressing affair. When people who do not want to give away anything, give to their pastor things which he does not want, the ceremony does not promote hilarity. In order to render the donation party somewhat less gloomy than a funeral those who bring gifts usually include among them a supply of cake, sandwiches, and in some cases ice-cream. These refreshments are distributed in equal proportion between the interior of the visitors and the exterior of the minister's carpets and chair-cushions, and a hollow pretence of cheerfulness is thus kept up. Meanwhile, all the children of the congregation retire to the second-story front bed-room, where they play various games and break a good deal of furniture. The children have much the best of the whole affair, and they add materially to the anguish of the minister's wife, as she wonders how many of them will fall against the stove, and whether they will set the house on fire when they upset the lamp.

The peculiar character of Rev. Mr. WILCOX's recent donation party and the unfortunate results which followed it, were due solely to his small-boy's disgust at being forbidden to take part in the juvenile cake orgies of the party. A week before the date fixed for the annual visit to the pastor, this small-boy had been detected in the act of creeping into his bedroom window at midnight, after a secret visit to the circus. The ensuing interview with his father did not materially depress his spirits, since he took the precaution to plate the vital portion of his trousers with concealed shingles, but when he was sternly told that, as a further penalty, he would be put to bed at precisely six o'clock on the night of the donation party, he felt that his punishment was inhuman, and resolved to be revenged.

During the next six days that astute but fearfully depraved small-boy called upon every one of his father's parishioners, and first pledging them to secrecy, explained, with tears in his eyes, that his dear father was passionately fond of cabbages, and if any one desired to gladden the parental heart they would bring a few cabbages to the donation party. The small-boy further asserted that his father's sense of delicacy forbade him to make the most distant allusion to cabbages, but that as an affectionate son, he—the small-boy—felt it to be his duty to mention the matter to some noble and generous man. Each parishioner was delighted by this display of filial affection and the recollection that cabbages were extremely cheap, and unhesitatingly promised that he would bring a whole load of cabbages.

The night of the donation party arrived, and the small-boy went to bed but not to sleep. With much forethought he had stolen the key of his bedroom, and thus rendered it impossible for his father to keep him a close prisoner. Each parishioner arrived in a large farm wagon, which, after

having discharged its human freight at the front
door was driven into the yard.   The minister and
his wife did not, of course, know the contents of
the wagons, but supposing that the popular feeling
was expressing itself to an unprecedented extent
in wood, flour-barrels, and winter apples, were
greatly delighted. At 8:30 sixty-three wagons had
entered the yard, and only three pecks of beans
and eleven pen-wipers had been deposited on the
parlor table.   The happy minister was beginning
to think that at least twenty cords of wood, together with say a dozen barrels of flour, must have
been delivered in the back yard, when suddenly
his small-boy, confident that he would not be punished in public, entered the parlor and exclaimed
in an exulting tone : " Father, there's morenamil-
lion loads of cabbage out-doors."   At this moment
the sixty-fourth wagon arrived, and the owner,
Deacon Lyman, put his head in the front door and
remarked that he " had brought a few cabbages,
but see'n as the yard was chock full, he calculated

he might as well dump them under the front windows."

The alarmed minister went out hastily, and beheld a mountain of cabbages. There was not a stick of wood, nor a barrel of flour, nor a bushel of apples in sight. Sixty-three full loads of cabbages were piled up nearly to the second-story windows of the parsonage, and Deacon Lyman was just about to add his contingent to the pile. With a stern and angry countenance Mr. Wilcox went back to his parlor, and coldly informing his guests that to make a jest of sacred things in his own back yard was an insult which he could not pardon, bade them good-night and withdrew to the recesses of a back bedroom. The guests, in their turn filled with indignation at his apparent ingratitude and rudeness, went to their homes and determined to change their minister at the earliest opportunity, and the depraved small-boy, after gorging himself with cake, went chuckling to his room and stood on his head in ecstatic bliss. The cabbages have since been sold at three cents per dozen, the minister has resigned his charge, and the small-boy, having too late perceived the ruin he had wrought, is now earnestly hoping that the doctrine of Universalism may be true.

VERY POPULAR SCIENCE.

OF late years there has grown up a large demand for what is called "popular science," or, in other words, a presentation of the facts of science in terms intelligible to the uncultured public. Scores of lecturers and hundreds of writers have endeavored, with more or less success, to popularize science, and their labors have been warmly appreciated. As a result, almost every man who knows how to read knows that the sun is some distance from the earth; that the cold of winter is caused by a diminution of heat; that the earth and most of the South American Republics complete one revolution every year, together with various other interesting scientific facts. It is remarkable, however, that in spite of all that has been said upon the subject, the new doctrine in regard to heat is yet very far from being generally comprehended. When scientific persons taught that heat was an invisible substance, the presence of which in any given object made it warm, while its absence made the same object cold, there was no difficulty in understanding the matter. Now, however, when people are told that this theory is all wrong, and that heat is a mode of motion, they fail to understand what is meant. There is so much ignorance and misapprehension in regard to this subject that a familiar and lucid exposition of the true theory of heat ought to be generally useful and acceptable to our readers.

Heat is a mode of motion. In order to understand this definition we must know what motion is, and according to the best authorities motion is a correlative of heat. To make the matter clearer to the Western mind it may be said that motion is a sort of interconvertible currency that can be always exchanged for heat, while, in its turn, heat can be converted into motion. Having thus shown in the clearest possible manner what heat is, we can proceed to prove the truth of the definition by experiments.

Friction, it will be conceded, is motion, and it infallibly produces heat if it is kept up long enough. Thus, if we take a scientific person and rub his hair with great violence, we produce a brilliant display of heated temper. In this case, just as in the more familiar and less scientific experiment of rubbing a match on the wall, motion is converted into heat. The law illustrated by this experiment is universal and admits of no exceptions. If you take a slab of water, say two inches thick, six inches wide and a foot long, and placing it on a common dining-table, rub it vigorously with sand-paper, it will ultimately be brought to the boiling point, or in other words the motion of the sand-paper over its surface will be converted into heat. In like manner, the human boot, if brushed long enough, will be calcined with the heat set free by the movement of the brush, to such an extent that it will be undistinguishable from the beefsteak of commerce which is familiar to the inmates of an American boarding-house. An unlimited number of experiments of the same general nature may be tried, with a uniform result. Thus, we see that the mode of motion called friction is always convertible into heat, just as a Western debtor is convertible into an advocate of the Silver bill.

There is another class of experiments which shows that motion, when suddenly arrested, is instantaneously changed into heat. If a cannon ball strikes an iron target, the latter immediately becomes hot. In fact, a blow always produces heat, or, in other words, the motion inseparable from a blow is always converted into heat. The experiments which illustrate this are of exceptional interest. If you take a cold foot, whether your own or some one else's—though this experiment is more conclusive if the foot is your own—and strike it a series of heavy blows with a large hammer or the back of an axe, the foot will become warm. Of course, a single blow may not develop a very appreciable amount of heat, but if the experiment is continued for some time, and the hammer or axe is used vigorously, the foot will soon cease to feel cold. A similar experiment is often tried by a school-teacher with the aid of a small-boy and a club. When the latter is applied to the former with force and rapidity, the boy becomes thoroughly warm— whence we have the popular juvenile expression descriptive of this kind of experiment, " the teacher just everlastingly warmed him, you bet " !

The important fact that heat is developed by suddenly arrested motion might be applied to various useful purposes were it generally known. Eggs can be cooked without fire simply by pounding them with a hammer until sufficient heat is developed to fry them nicely. Furnaces, grates, and stoves could be dispensed with were the members of every family to provide themselves with the old-fashioned flails formerly in use among farmers, and to thrash one another, together with the walls and furniture of their houses, until the thermometer should indicate a pleasant and healthful temperature. In fact, if you have motion enough, you can produce any amount of heat, or if you have heat enough, you can produce any amount of motion; of which latter fact the familiar experiment of kindling a straw fire under a balky horse affords a convincing illustration.

Had Professor TYNDALL and his fellow-lecturers presented the new theory of heat in a clear and intelligible way, it would not have been necessary to thus put them to the blush.   Still, it is unendurable that the public should be ignorant of the grand doctrine of the correlation of forces, and the scientific persons ought not to feel jealous if our explanation leaves them nothing further to explain.

A SLEIGHING TRAGEDY.

MR. JOHNSTON, of North Lyme, Connecti-
cut, is an upright man, and in many respects a wise one. He is, however, weak enough
to imagine that he can keep his pretty daughter
from all amusements except the weekly prayer-
meeting and the annual donation party. The
amusements in which young girls delight, no matter how innocent they may be in the eyes of other
men, Mr. Johnston summarily condemns as vain
and frivolous. Of course, this line of conduct cannot be commended, but it is, nevertheless, true
that Miss Johnston ought to obey the commands
of her father while she is yet in her minority and
under his roof. It is painful to be compelled to
mention that such is not the view of the matter
taken by the spirited and undutiful girl. While
she does not venture to openly defy the author of

her existence, she does not hesitate to deceive him. She snatches surreptitious joys whenever the paternal back is turned, and such is her versatility that she has been known to entertain three distinct and simultaneous young men—one in the woodshed, another at the back gate, and a third under the lilac-bush in the front yard, at the very time when Mr. Johnston fondly imagined that she was in her room studying the Shorter Catechism by lamp-light. The neighbors, from sympathy with youth and beauty subjected to parental tyranny, assist her in her undutiful conduct, and conceal from her unsuspecting father her indulgence in picnics and skating parties.

Among the young lady's warmest admirers is the young man who presides over the local public school. He is an unexceptionable person, except in point of muscle. He is not strong, and he is not familiar with out-of-door sports. Still, these faults do not affect his moral character, and most certainly did not justify Mr. Johnston in leading him out of the house by his left ear on the solitary occasion on which he had rashly ventured to call on the, stern old gentleman's daughter. As was only natural, this want of delicacy and hospitality exasperated the school-teacher, and though, as he afterward explained to a friend who happened to be passing the house at the moment when the pedagogical ear was undergoing undue familiarity, he did not feel at liberty to inflict personal chastisement upon Miss Johnston's father, he was, nevertheless, determined to "get square" with him, let the consequences be what they might.

A few weeks later the first heavy fall of snow occurred in North Lyme, and Mr. Parker—for that was the school-teacher's name—determined to invite Miss Johnston to accompany him on a sleigh-ride. He knew that she would be delighted to accept an invitation, and that her father regarded sleigh-riding as one of the worst vices in which his daughter could possibly indulge. To please himself and the young lady and to triumph over her objectionable parent, presented itself to his mind as a delicious combination of pleasure and revenge,

8

and accordingly he wrote to Miss Johnston to meet
him in a quiet lane a short distance from the village, and proceeded to the livery stable to hire a
sleigh.

Mr. Parker was not, as the event proved, a
judge of sleighs. Moreover, there was just at that
time an excessive demand upon the resources of
the livery stable, and every sleigh but one was engaged. This one was an aged " cutter " of a de-
cidedly rickety appearance, but Mr. Parker found
no fault with it, and, after hiring a horse warranted
to be old and gentle, he entered the sleigh and
drove cautiously to the rendezvous. Miss Johnston, with her cheeks and nose glowing with frost
and expectation, was waiting for him, and his
heart beat high as he alighted and prepared to
assist her to the seat.

A surfeit of small-boys and a prolonged course
of boarding-house beefsteak had reduced Mr. Parker's weight to 103 pounds,—as he afterward
testified before the Justice of the Peace. Miss
Johnston, on the other hand, was a plump young

person, who weighed 139 pounds without her back
hair. The sleigh had borne the school-teacher,
though with much ominous creaking, but it was
unequal to the strain of 139 pounds of girl. As
Miss Johnston stepped into the middle of the
" cutter," and paused to arrange her skirts with a
view to sitting down, a sharp crackling sound was
heard, and the unhappy girl suddenly went through
the bottom, and was held fast by cruel splinters,
with her feet just touching the snow.

Mr. Parker rushed to the rescue with the utmost promptness, and mounting on the seat, strove
to extricate his companion from the wreck; but
the inexorable splinters would not yield. He
tried to break the entire bottom out of the sleigh,
but his strength was unequal to the feat. With
rare inventive genius, he next proposed to crawl
under the sleigh to extricate Miss Johnston by
cutting away the splinters with his knife, but she
declared with vigorous eloquence that if he dared
to even bend his head down she would never speak
to him again the longest day she lived. Just at

this point the horse showed signs of restlessness,
and the young lady insisted that the animal should
be instantly cast loose from the sleigh, lest his
movements should further complicate her misfortune.   Accordingly, the horse was sent adrift, and
the discouraged Mr. Parker was left alone with
his weeping companion, who constantly upbraided
him, and as constantly refused all his offers of
assistance.

At the end of half an hour Miss Johnston began
to suffer from the cold, and as she firmly refused
to allow a blanket to be wrapped around—that is
to say, to be placed in position beneath the sleigh,
the situation became alarming.   Finally, Mr. Parker
hit upon the idea of gently dragging the sleigh,
while the imprisoned fair one feebly imitated the
movement of walking.   This gentle exercise prevented her from freezing, but it was obviously impossible for her to enter the village in such an unprecedented style, and she actually hailed with
delight the sudden appearance of her father, in
connection with a load of wood.   That gentleman

was naturally surprised at the spectacle which he beheld, but he was wrong in characterizing it as a wicked and willful attempt to play at circus.

Mr. Johnston, with the help of his whip, convinced the school-teacher that he had better hasten home; and he then extricated his daughter, by summarily knocking the sleigh to pieces. He has since sued Mr. Parker for damages inflicted upon Miss Johnston by means of splinters and exposure to the weather, and though the case has not yet been decided, it is generally thought that the plaintiff will succeed. The story is a very sad one, and is well adapted to awaken within us a variety of painful, though salutary, emotions.

THE MANAGING YOUNG MAN.

THIS world is full of painful duties which are constantly assigned to the conscientious journalist. Close upon the sleigh-riding tragedy at North Lyme comes the news of a still more appalling incident of sleighing in New Jersey, which demands to be delicately, yet firmly, set before the public. It is not the journalist's fault that these things happen. It has long been the opinion of thoughtful men that the constant tendency of things to happen ought to be checked; but alas! we are as yet powerless to check it. Every man will wish that the tragedy which it now becomes necessary to relate had never occurred, but regrets are useless. We can only strive to draw from it lessons that may teach us to guard against similar calamities, and that may sustain and strengthen us in moments of heated anguish.

The whole responsibility of the affair belongs to a young man whose name it would be an unnecessary act of cruelty to mention. It is out of regard to this well-meaning but unfortunate person that the name of the New Jersey village in which the tragedy occurred is not here specified. It is sufficient to say that he was regarded as an expert in young ladies, and had won universal female gratitude by his intelligent efforts to please the sex. When, therefore, he undertook to manage what in the New Jersey dialect is called a " straw sleigh-ride," it was generally believed that the success of the affair was already assured.

The essential ingredients of a " straw sleigh-ride " are from fifteen to twenty-five young men and women, a large box sleigh without seats, and a quantity of straw. The straw is strewn in the bottom of the sleigh, and the pleasure-seekers sit on the straw, leaning their respective backs against the sides of the sleigh. Of course, they are uncomfortable, but the sense of doing something unusual and unconventional gives a zest to a straw sleigh-ride which renders it immensely popular with the young. There is, however, one serious drawback to the pleasure of such an excursion. The cold air will penetrate through the bottom of the sleigh in spite of the straw, and will exercise a chilling influence upon the mirth and the geniality of the party. On this particular occasion the Managing Young Man undertook to provide means for keeping the young ladies thoroughly warm, and the latter placed unreserved confidence in his wisdom and skill.

Everybody knows that bricks when thoroughly heated and wrapped up in paper will preserve their warmth for many hours. The Managing Young Man determined to warm the young ladies of the sleighing party with bricks, and by an elaborate calculation arrived at the conclusion that each young lady would require four bricks. As the party was to consist of eleven girls and seven young men, he laid in no less than forty-four bricks, all of which he heated for several hours in the furnace of the Town Hall, and subsequently placed in the bottom of the sleigh, having first neatly wrapped them in copies of the *Tribune* so that the girls might feel thoroughly at home while sitting on them.

At about 8 o'clock in the evening the sleigh received its precious freight, and the Managing Young Man was overwhelmed with thanks for his thoughtful conduct in protecting the young ladies from cold. The heat from the bricks was at first exceedingly welcome, but after a time a certain uneasiness on the part of the young ladies was manifested. They conversed in an absent-minded and preoccupied manner, and evinced that constant tendency to uneasy movements which is said by scientific persons to characterize a hen when placed on a hot griddle, although there is no authentic record that any such brutal experiment has ever been tried. A little later and the girls abandoned all attempts to join in general conversation, and whispered to one another with every appearance of anxiety and alarm. . Presently they began with one accord to grope nervously and stealthily in the

8*

straw, and several of them suddenly shrieked and blew violently upon their fingers. At last the astonished Managing Young Man was unanimously called upon with frenzied energy to instantly stop the sleigh, and as soon as the order was obeyed the young ladies sprang out with a haste that disdained any masculine assistance.

The smell of singed paper had by this time suggested an explanation of the mystery, and the demand which was presently made that every brick should be thrown out of the sleigh left no further room for doubt in the mind of the Managing Young Man. He burned his fingers severely while handling the overheated bricks, but he cared not for his own physical pain. The thought that instead of making the girls comfortable he had inflicted upon them the tortures of St. LAWRENCE, filled him with humiliation. The girls were merely human, and it was natural that they should feel extremely dissatisfied with him, but it was scarcely just for them to refuse to accept his apologies and to treat him with cold disdain. The conduct of one particular young lady, whom he ardently admired, and whom he had secretly provided with an extra brick, pierced him to the heart. She persistently sat on a snow-bank, and refused to be comforted or to concede that he was not a hateful, unfeeling brute. When the cargo of bricks' was finally thrown out and the girls resumed their places in the sleigh, the whole pleasure of the excursion was manifestly wrecked, and the Managing Young Man, who had exiled himself to the driver's seat, felt that he was a combination of half a dozen distinct and infamous kinds of criminals.

It is all over now. The young ladies have recovered their spirits, and would perhaps forgive. the Managing Young Man were he to return and sue for forgiveness. But he is far away, having fled the village and buried himself in the wilds of Chicago. May his fate be a warning to us all, and may we remember that, though a warm brick has its uses, there may be too much of a good thing.

SEDENTARY ABILITIES.

PRESIDENT BASCOM, who presides over a Western college to which young ladies, as well as young men, are admitted, has recently expressed his warm approval of the co-education of the sexes and has asserted that girls are better students than boys, for the reason that they are better adapted to sedentary pursuits. In other words, he claims that girls can sit down more successfully than boys, and that this fact enables them to surpass the other sex in study and in whatever business or profession involves a large amount of sitting down. Far be it from us to dispute the learned President's facts. Doubtless he knows whereof he affirms, and we should cheerfully concede that the members of the gentler sex are unequaled in the capacity for sitting down. Still, the inferences which President BASCOM draws from this fact are not necessarily true. A person, of whatever sex, may be able to sit down to an immense extent and may, nevertheless, be wholly unable to study. The professional fat man and fat woman spend the greater part of their lives in the sedentary occupation of being looked at and pinched by curious people, but they have never, in a single instance, been noted for scholarship. As for the theory that because girls are peculiarly adapted to rocking-chairs they should therefore be admitted to young men's colleges, there is abundant reason why we should unhesitatingly reject it.

While girls unquestionably have their uses in the economy of nature, and possess merits exclusively their own, it may be boldly asserted that they are totally unfit to pursue in company with young men the studies which constitute the curriculum of every respectable college. One of the earliest studies of the Freshman year is the art of getting the janitor's cow into the fourth story of the dormitory. This can be readily mastered by any young man of good abilities and habits of industry and perseverance; but between girls and cows there is a great gulf fixed. The girl, from her earliest youth, looks upon the cow as a ferocious beast, prone to keep young ladies in the air in positions. fatal to the proper arrangement of the back hair. To suppose that three or four young lady students are capable of the complicated pushing and pulling necessary to induce a cow to climb several flights of stairs, is to suppose that the natural feminine fear of cows can be eradicated by the mere process of matriculation. Thus we see that one of the very easiest of college studies is quite beyond the range of the female intellect.

The Sophomore year in most of our colleges is devoted to base-ball. Will President Bascom have the temerity to assert that this is a sedentary pursuit, or that it is one in which it is possible for girls to excel? We all know that nature has so constructed the girl that she cannot throw a ball with any force or accuracy. If the most accomplished of President Bascom's young ladies were to attempt to pitch a base-ball, the chances are that,

instead of coming within reach of the batsman, it
would describe a parabolic curve and smash the
President's front window. Nor can young lady
students strike or catch a ball when thrown with
the proper degree of force. In short, base-ball is a
study in which it is morally impossible that girls
should ever successfully compete with men. The
same may be said of foot-ball, which, in some
colleges, is an optional study, which those who do
not fancy base-ball are permitted to substitute for
the latter. It is barely possible, judging from the
remarks which Chicago and St. Louis newspapers
constantly make in regard to the feet of the ladies
of those cities, that Western girls are better adapted
for foot-ball than are the girls this side of the Alle-
ghanies, but it may be safely asserted that no girl
can graduate in foot-ball, especially in colleges
where the Rugby method is studied, with any.
honor, or, indeed, with any high standing in her
class. By far the most important study pursued
at any American college is that of rowing. From
this study girls are virtually debarred simply by

reason of their sex. Man is so constituted that he can reduce his clothing to a close-fitting undershirt and a pair of attenuated trousers, which add scarcely anything to his weight in a six-oared shell. It is asserted by all scientific authorities that girls are incased in many successive layers of clothing, which are believed to be permanently affixed to them, and the aggregate weight of which is enormous. This would alone render girls unfit to pursue the fascinating and improving study of rowing, but there are other obstacles equally impossible to be overcome. Girls cannot run to any extent worth mentioning; and are hence unable to run along the shore while a boat-race is in progress, yelling encouragement to the oarsmen, and announcing the odds which they are prepared to bet upon their favorite crews. Nor are they able to vie with the other sex in making hideous the night after the race. Perhaps they would submit to the deprivation of caramels and the total abstinence from tea which are necessary while undergoing training, but what plump young lady would be willing to reduce herself to a gaunt and sun-burned oarswoman, even in order to beat the Yale or the Columbia crew? It might also be mentioned that a race is rowed principally with the muscles of the oarsmen's legs, and it is well known that the gentler sex—But this is, perhaps, a branch of the subject which can be discussed with proper delicacy only by a convention of strong-minded women.

In several of the minor studies of the college course, such as euchre, the amputation of the clapper of the chapel bell, the nailing up of the tutor's door, and the introduction of goats and other comparatively innocuous animals into the recitation room, girls may very possibly be able to maintain something like an equality with boys. Still, enough has been said to show that they are very far from being adapted to pursue those more important studies which convert the industrious undergraduate into a healthy, earnest, learned, and Christian man. What, then, does President Bascom mean by his assuming that merely because girls can sit down rather more than boys, they are peculiarly adapted to pursue the regular studies of the Yale and Columbia students ?

CAT FISHING.

CAT-FISHING.

MANY and ingenious are the remedies that have been proposed for nocturnal cats, but none of them seem to have proved thoroughly successful. It was pointed out not very long ago that the extirpation of all fences which run in a direction parallel, or nearly parallel, with the equator, would exempt cats from electrical difficulties in their internal organs, and would thus hush the cries that now render night hideous; but there is a practical difficulty in dispensing with these fences. Another remedy, which is a certain cure for nocturnal cats, is suggested by the fact that cats cannot live at a greater elevation than 13,000 feet above the sea. If we build our back fences 13,500 feet high, not a cat will scale their lofty summits; but the labor and expense of constructing fences of this height would be so great as to forbid their erection by persons of small incomes. Mere palliatives, such as boot-

jacks and lumps of coal, never accomplish any
lasting benefit; they may discourage an occasional
cat, but his place will instantly be filled. With
all their habitual caution, cats are bold, and will
often rush in where an average angel would fear to
tread. To deal effectually with them is a task
which calls for the highest form of inventive genius,
combined with patience and a reckless indifference
to Mr. BERGH's opinions.

The young man in West Thirty-fifth street who
lately introduced cat-fishing as a manly and beneficent sport, can scarcely be said to have devised
an absolute specific for cats, but he has unquestionably contributed to lessen the number of cats in
his immediate vicinity. Early last fall a vast
area of cats, accompanied with marked depression
of the spirits of the inhabitants of West Thirty-fifth
street, overspread that unfortunate region. After
a thorough trial of most of the popular remedies, a
young man residing on the block between Fifth and
Sixth avenues, and who may be called—not necessarily for publication, but as a guarantee of good

faith—by the name of Thompson, hit upon the idea of angling for cats. To the end of a strong blue-fish line he affixed a salmon-hook, baited with delicate morsels of meat. At first, this hook, deftly dropped from a back window, was permitted to lie on the top of the back fence. The first cat that passed over the fence would investigate the bait, and, finding it apparently free from fraud, would begin to eat it. A slight pull at the line would usually fix the hook in the cat's mouth, and the angler would haul in his prey and knock it on the head. It frequently happened, however, that the cat could not be successfully " struck," and would escape and warn his associates to beware of concealed hooks. Moreover, the angler had his bait gorged, upon one occasion, by a tramp, who had climbed the fence with a view to gaining access to the kitchen, and, though the game was successfully landed in the second-story back room, after having been gaffed with a sword bayonet, he had so much difficulty in subsequently disposing of the body that he dreaded a repetition of the incident. He therefore altered his method of angling, and adopted a modified style of fly-fishing.

This latter sport was carried on with the aid of a long bamboo fishing-pole. The hook was baited as before, but instead of being permitted to lie on the top of the fence, was suffered to dangle in the air, about two feet above it. As soon as a cat perceived the bait, he assumed, with the intense self-conceit characteristic of his race, that it was a supernatural recognition of his extraordinary merits, and could be fearlessly appropriated. In order to seize it he was, of course, compelled to leap upward, and it was very seldom that he failed to hook himself. By this plan, not only was the necessity of "striking" the cat obviated, but the danger that the bait would be seized by tramps was greatly lessened, while the excitement and interest of the sport were increased.

The young man became greatly fascinated with his new occupation, and having effected an arrangement with a popular French restaurant, was enabled to dispose of his game easily and profitably.

On moonlight nights, when the late fall cats were in season, he often caught a string of from three to four dozen during a single night, many of them weighing ten or fifteen pounds each. So few cats, escaped after having once leaped at the bait, that no general suspicion of the deadly nature of apparently aerial meat was disseminated among the feline population of the neighborhood. Before the winter was over cats had become so scarce that the sportsman was seriously contemplating the necessity of artificially stocking the back fences of Thirty-fifth-street, when an unfortunate accident brought his beneficent occupation to a sudden end. An old gentleman, residing in a house on Thirty-sixth street, the back yard of which adjoined the fence where the young man practised his sport, noticed one evening that something attached to a string was dangling over his back fence. As he had a pretty daughter, he immediately suspected that it was a surreptitious note, and stole softly out to seize and confiscate it. Mounting on a barrel he clutched the supposed note, and was instantly hooked.

The tackle was strong, and he would perhaps have been landed had not the hook torn out when he was about forty feet from the ground. After he had recovered from the injuries caused by the fall and the weakness consequent upon the amputation of his legs, he showed so much annoyance at the so-called outrage which had been inflicted upon him, that the young man, who was a person of the most delicate feelings, promised to give up cat-fishing. Of course, had the old gentleman been thoroughly gaffed, he would not have fallen, and perhaps the young man felt that his failure to gaff him was an inexcusable error, which really called for his graceful retirement from cat-fishing.

This example ought to bear fruit. At a very small expense for tackle, any resident of this city who occupies a back room, can secure excellent sport, and at the same time can render a great service to humanity by reducing the number of cats. The sport ought speedily to become a very popular one, and there can be but little doubt that in time cat-fishing will rival trout-fishing in the estimation of American sportsmen.

A MOURNFUL INCIDENT.

THE temperance crusade in Georgetown, Michigan, which was carried on by the earnest women of the village last winter, was a great success. When the crusade began there were five "saloons," at which various immoral beverages, from mild lager-beer to fiery benzine whisky, were sold, but before spring only one of the "saloonkeepers" insulted female public sentiment by continuing to prosecute his business. Of the others, three had sold out their entire stock to the crusaders, at a profit of nearly 200 per cent., and had removed to the next town, where they opened larger and more attractive "saloons;" while the fourth reformed rum-seller openly repented for $750 cash, and became a temperance lecturer, at $50 a night, which, together with his income from a gambling-house, made him very comfortable. In

9

fact, he was accustomed to say that, as between
selling liquor for a profit of $800 a year, and prac-
ticing as a reformer for $11,000 a year, no intelligent
man could hesitate to choose the latter, and that
he hoped in the course of a few months to find an
opening as a reformed gambler that would make
his fortune at one blow.

The one obdurate liquor-dealer was without
doubt one of the most exasperating ruffians on
record.   Night after night did the devoted women
of Georgetown enter his "saloon" and hold a
prayer-meeting of great size and strength, but he
never once openly insulted them, so as to enable
the male crusaders to smash his bottles about his
ears.   On the contrary, he provided a parlor-organ
and six dozen hymn-books, and joined in the singing with great ardor.   When he was personally
exhorted to give up his nefarious business, he
always expressed a great desire to reform, but
fixed his price at $3,000, which was considered to
be altogether too high.   It was useless to labor
with such a hardened reprobate, and after six

months of unremitting effort, the earnest women shook his sawdust from their feet and abandoned the attempt to reform him. When he was told that no more prayer-meetings would be held in his " saloon," he expressed sincere regret, and offered to reform for only $2,500, but even this offer was rejected, and then, for the first time, he lost his temper, and remarked that people who refused to save an immortal soul and put an end to drunkenness at the low price of $2,500 were insincere, and should no longer pollute his premises with their hypocritical prayers. In spite of this one failure, the crusaders had accomplished so much that, on the 23d of November last, the anniversary of the formation of the " Earnest Women's Anti Rum, Beer and Tobacco League," they determined to celebrate the occasion by a public procession and a cold water festival in the Baptist meeting-house. The procession was to march in front of the obdurate liquor-seller's " saloon," with any quantity of banners—the Earnest Women singing temperance hymns, thus dispensing with the services of a beer-

drinking German brass band.   When the "saloon"
keeper heard of the intended celebration, he smiled
grimly, and announced that if the procession did
not halt in front of his "saloon," he should feel
personally slighted.

Now, the sidewalk in front of that wicked
man's "saloon" was wide and was paved with a
peculiar mixture of tar and gravel.   It was slightly
out of repair, and the liquor-seller remarked that
he should show his respect for the temperance
cause by having it put in complete repair.   He,
however, postponed the work from day to day,
until it was generally thought that he had abandoned his design, but on the very night before the
procession a gang of men, with lanterns and tar
barrels, appeared on the scene, and before daylight
the sidewalk was finished.   In the morning two
sentinels were stationed to warn pedestrians not to
step on the newly laid pavement, which, however,
the liquor-dealer asserted would be perfectly hard
before the hour fixed for the procession.

It was nearly 11 o'clock before the Earnest

Women, singing a powerful hymn and carrying more banners than a torch-light political procession, turned the corner and advanced toward the "saloon." The two sentinels were hastily withdrawn, and the liquor-seller, with his hat in his hand, stood at his doorway to do homage to the reformers. As they neared him they averted their gaze, and would have passed him without recognizing his existence, but, unfortunately, the procession, instead of passing his door, halted before it, and standing perfectly still, ceased singing, and remarked with great unanimity "goodness gracious," and other words to the same general effect.

Contrary to the prediction of the liquor-seller, the new pavement was not dry. The composition had been spread to the unusual depth of six inches, and the head of the procession, including twenty-six Earnest Women, was securely stuck in the adhesive compound. To lift their feet was an impossibility, and two ladies who rashly sat down with the view of removing their boots, and thus

making their escape, found it impossible to rise
again. The wicked "saloon"-keeper at first pretended not to notice the misfortune which had befallen the procession, and assuming that the ladies
had paused for refreshments. loudly begged the
ladies " to name their poison and he would be delighted to supply them." Of course, he was soon
compelled to recognize the true cause of the stop-
page of the procession, and he then professed to·
be so overwhelmed with sorrow that he felt unable
to gaze upon the scene, and so put up his shutters
and retired by the back door into an adjoining
street.

The Earnest Women were ultimately pried out
with fence rails, after hot crowbars had been used
to soften the tenacious tar, and they were then
taken home in carriages and scraped by their devoted husbands. The affair, however, cast a gloom
over the reformers and seriously injured the cause.
The. wicked liquor-dealer had a sudden increase of
custom, and it is understood that two new saloons
are to be opened at an early day. This melan-

choly event may well fill us with sorrow, while it conveys the solemn lesson that reformers should take heed to their footsteps, lest haply they fall into the snares of the wicked.

DOGS AND GHOSTS.

IT is all very well to be a philosopher and to make all sorts of investigations with all sorts of things; but when it comes to trifling with the holiest feelings of an honest Scotch terrier, under the pretext of investigating his religious views, it is time that prying philosophers should be told to exercise some little self-restraint and decency.

M. COMTE, the philosopher who invented an ingenious religion, based upon the cheerful and sustaining doctrines that there is no GOD and that the soul is not immortal, held that dogs have a religion closely resembling fetichism. An English philosopher, one Mr. GEORGE J. ROMANES, who is evidently on intimate terms with dogs, but who is obviously undeserving of that precious privilege, has recently been investigating the alleged fetichism of dogs, and has decided that while they are

not really fetich-worshipers, they are firm believers in ghosts and spiritualism. It is not with Mr. Romanes' conclusions that we need find fault, but with his methods of investigation. That prying and indelicate person arrived at his alleged facts by a series of experiments upon a Skye terrier of culture and refinement, which, if generally known in polite dog circles, would subject him to severe barking, if not to actual biting.

His first experiment was made with a bone. This is alone sufficient to show the heartless and irreverent character of the man. If there is any thing which a dog holds peculiarly sacred, it is a bone. A terrier will submit to be deluded by false representations that there are eligible cats in the coal-scuttle, or that the piano is full of rats, but he feels that bones are too sacred to be made the subject of jest. But what did Mr. Romanes do? According to his own confession, he tied a small silk thread to a bone and gave it to a dog. After that animal had convinced himself that it was in all respects a genuine and substantial bone, the philosopher possessed himself of the end of the thread and drew the bone slowly across the floor. The astonished dog watched the unprecedented spectacle of an apparently self-moving bone with startled ears and terrified tail until he convinced himself that he was not dreaming, **but that a** ghostly bone had materialized itself in front of his nose. When this conviction had mastered his mind, he fled, howling and with every symptom of terror, to his kennel, where he undoubtedly spent a miserable night, torturing himself with inquiries as to what this supernatural appearance might portend, and whether he had committed some grave sin in point of cats or rats for which the vision of the ghostly bone was intended as a punishment.

Mr. ROMANES argues from this cruel experiment that his dog recognizes the existence of supernatural things and dreads them. Of course, the philosopher fails to notice that the conduct of the dog was far more sensible than is the conduct of the average man who thinks he sees something supernatural. In all probability had Mr. ROMANES ever seen a piece of roast beef in the act of cruising unassisted around the table, he would instantly have asked it preposterous questions, and would subsequently have let his hair grow long, and have become a confirmed Spiritualist. His intelligent dog did none of these things, but as soon as he decided that he had seen a spiritual bone, he refused to have anything more to do with it, and continued to wear his hear of the usual length, and to cling to that faith in which he was educated. Still, although the experiment proved that the dog was far superior to his master, it was a cruel trifling with the most sacred feelings of his canine soul, and the philosopher deserves to be classed with the scarcely less cruel and far less mischievous practitioners of vivisection.

Not content with his first experiment, Mr. ROMANES tried another. He blew soap-bubbles, suffered them to roll along the carpet, and called his dog's attention to them. It took some time to convince the dog that they were not a new kind of particularly dangerous rat, but he ultimately made up his mind to attack them. The first bubble upon which he placed his paw instantly vanished, much to his amazement. However, he was not easily discouraged, and he attacked a second bubble with a similar result. Then there flashed upon him the recollection of the ghostly bone, and he decided that soap-bubbles were also supernatural. Again he fled, manifesting every symptom of extreme terror, and has never since consented to remain in a room in company with even the smallest bubble.

Finally, Mr. ROMANES tried the dignified experiment of "making faces" at his unfortunate dog. Whether he is a handsome man in his normal state or not, he refrains from informing us, but it is certain that he made his face so hideously ugly that the dog mistook him for a worse ghost than any he had yet seen, and thereupon crept under the sofa and tried to die. A world abounding in supernatural bones and soap-bubbles, and infested with an atrocious demon in the clothes, though not the likeness, of his master, had no further charms for him, and he preferred to leave it, and to hunt the unsubstantial cats of the other world, in the appropriate character of an unsubstantial and ghostly dog.

If that outraged dog had as little generosity as the average man, he would tell his miserable tale to all his acquaintances, and enlist their sympathies in his behalf. If this were done Mr. Romanes would be fitly punished. Avenging dogs would lie in wait for him at every corner and bite his sacrilegious legs. They would take turns in howling before his midnight windows, until the lack of sleep would drive him into insanity, and they would finally convert his grave into a canine base-ball ground. He ought not, however, to be left exclusively to the vengeance of the dogs. He has done his best to disseminate among dogs a belief in ghosts which tends to unfit them for the duties of their station. This is a direct injury to every dog-owner, and Mr. Romanes should not be permitted to lead our dogs into evil ways with impunity.

RED HAIR.

THE name of the lady who a few weeks since dropped her back hair on the sidewalk of a street in Clinton, Illinois, has never been ascertained. The hair in question was of a bright red color, and few persons imagined that it was dangerous when unconnected with its owner. Nevertheless, that seemingly innocent back hair led to a tragedy that nearly ruined the peace of two happy and respectable families.

Messrs. Smith and Brown are two leading citizens engaged in the grocery business in Clinton. They are men of great worth of character, and have reached middle age without incurring the breath of slander. One evening Mr. Smith returned from the store and sitting down at the tea-table, produced a Chicago paper from his pocket and remarked with much indignation, "That revolting

Beecher scandal has been revived, and its loathsome details are again polluting the press and cor-
rupting the minds of the public."

. Mrs. Smith replied that "it was a shameful
outrage that the papers were allowed to publish
such disgusting things," and asked her husband
"which paper had the fullest account of the matter." That excellent man said that he believed the
Gazette contained more about it than any other
paper, and that after tea he would send one of the
boys to get a copy of it. His wife thanked him,
and was in the act of remarking that he was always
thoughtful and considerate, when the oldest boy
exclaimed, "Pa, you've got a long red hair on
your coat collar !"

A prompt investigation made by Mrs. Smith
confirmed the boy's accusation. There was an un-
mistakably female hair on the collar of Mr. Smith's
coat, and it was obtrusively red. Mr. Smith said
that it was a very extraordinary thing, and Mrs.
Smith also remarking "very extraordinary, indeed,"
in a dry, sarcastic voice, expressed deep disgust at

red hair, and a profound contempt for the " nasty creatures " who wore it.

About the same hour Mr. Brown was also seated at his tea-table, and was endeavoring to excuse himself to Mrs. Brown for having forgotten to bring home a paper. That lady, after having expressed the utmost indignation at the revival of the Beecher scandal, had asked for the paper in order to see who was dead and married, and was, of course, indignant because her husband had not brought it home. In the heat of the discussion she noticed a long red hair on Mr. Brown's coat-collar, and, holding it up before him, she demanded an explanation. In vain did Mr. Brown allege that he had not the least idea how the hair became attached to his collar. His wife replied that what he said was simply ridiculous. " Red hair don't blow round like thistle-down, and at your time of life, Mr. Brown, you ought to be ashamed of yourself. The less you say the better, but I can tell you that you can't deceive me. I'm not a member of Plymouth Church, and you can't make me believe that black is white."

Now, both Mr. Brown and Mr. Smith were perfectly innocent. Of course, they were annoyed by the remarks of their respective wives, but like sensible men, they avoided any unnecessary discussion of the painful topic. The next day they each brought home all the Chicago papers that contained any reference to the Beecher matter, and, as the papers were received by Mrs. Brown and Mrs. Smith with many protestations of the disgust which they felt at hearing any mention of the scandal, they naturally supposed that they had made peace. But marital suspicion once awakened is not easily put to sleep. While Mr. Brown was handing his wife the bundle of newspapers, she was closely scrutinizing his coat-collar, and, after she had laid the papers on her plate and told the children not to touch them, she quietly took two long red hairs from her unfortunate husband's coat, and held them solemnly before his face.

"Mary, I give you my solemn word," began the alarmed Mr. Brown; but he was not permitted to finish his sentence. "Don't say one word,"

exclaimed Mrs. Brown.   "Falsehoods won't help
you; I am a faithful and loving wife, and I'll have
you exposed and punished if there is any law in
Illinois."   Thus saying she gathered up her newspapers and rushing to her room, locked herself in.
It was not until later in the evening that Mrs.
Smith, as she was about to turn down her husband's
lamp, which was smoking, perceived that two red
hairs were attached to his shoulder.   She said
nothing, but after laying them on the table before
him, burst into tears and refused to be comforted
until Mr. Smith solemnly swore that he had not
seen a red-haired girl for months and years, and
offered to buy her a new parlor carpet the very
next day.

Of the two ladies, Mrs. Brown was much the
stronger and the more determined.   The next
evening, when Mr. Brown brought back from the
store no less than five red hairs on his coat-collar,
she broke a pie-plate over his head, and leaving him
weltering in dried apples, put on her bonnet and
left the house.   Mrs. Smith, on the same even-

ing, found four of the mysterious red hairs on her husband's coat, but she refrained from violence, and merely telling him that she would not believe in his innocence if he was to swear till he was black in the face, called loudly for her sainted mother, and was about to faint when Mrs. Brown burst into the room. Mr. Smith, like a wise man, fled from the scene, and the two ladies soon confided their wrongs to one another.

When Mr. Brown and Mr. Smith met the next day, the former confessed to the latter that he was in a terrible scrape. Confidence begat confidence, and they soon became convinced that they were the victims of a frightful conspiracy to which some unknown wearer of red back-hair was a party. Their distress was increased early in the afternoon by the appearance of their respective wives, who walked up and down the opposite side of the street for hours, each carrying a conspicuous rawhide, and evidently lying in wait for the imaginary red-haired woman. Messrs. Smith and Brown felt that they were ruined men, and that a tremendous scandal was about to overwhelm them. They even wished that they were dead.

About 4 o'clock P. M. Mrs. Smith clutched her companion's arm and bade her listen to a small-boy who was relating one of his recent crimes to a youthful companion. " I just picked up that there hair," remarked the wicked youth, " and put some of it on old Smith's and old Brown's coats; I kep' a puttin' of it on every day, and you just bet they ketched it from their old women when they went home. Smith, he's as solemnsanowl, and old Brown looks as if he was a goin' to be hung."

The remains of the boy were removed by the constable, and the Smith and Brown families are once more united and happy.

THE PERIODICITY OF STORIES.

NO intelligent man now doubts the Copernican theory. We know that the planets revolve around the sun, and that every satellite revolves around its own private planet. Still, mankind has been curiously slow to perceive that the law upon which the Copernican theory is based is of vastly wider application than astronomers suppose. All things do not literally revolve, but all things have their periodic times. For many years after the death of COPERNICUS it was imagined that the comets were exempt from the laws which govern the planets, and it is only within a few years that astronomers have discovered that the whole stellar universe is revolving around some central point. With the solitary exception of the seventeen-year locusts and certain forms of epidemic disease, the law of periodicity is universally believed to have no application to mundane affairs. Nevertheless, everything revolves, either actually or figuratively, around something .else, and has its set times for appearing and disappearing; and this great truth will yet be recognized by scientific persons, as well as by the small boys who have made a profound study of the orbits and periods of circuses.

Take, for example, the British drum-beat. DANIEL WEBSTER long ago announced the scientific fact that this drum-beat encircles the earth, and that its time of revolution is precisely that of the axial revolution of the earth. But who, among all our scientific persons, has noticed that the British drum-beat revolves not in the plane of the equator, but nearly in that of the ecliptic? Its path may be traced by a line drawn from Gibraltar, through Jamaica, British Guiana, and the Fiji Islands, to Australia, and thence bending northerly through India, Suez, and Malta to the place of beginning. It is idle to suppose that this a mere accident. Nature, which caused Greenwich to be placed pre- cisely equidistant between the first parallels of east and west longitude, knew what she was about when she ordained that the British drum-beat should circle the earth in a plane but slightly inclined to that of the ecliptic.

The appearance in a Chicago paper of the story of an alleged marriage ceremony which came to an abrupt end because the bride and groom mutually accused each other of awkwardness, furnishes a fitting occasion to call attention to the fact that all stories have their periodic times. The story in question was a popular one precisely twenty-six years ago, as will appear by an examination of the comic almanacs of the year 1851, and its reappearance at this time shows that its periodic time is, in round numbers, twenty-six years. The Chicago paper, ignorant of this fact, supposes that the story is a new one, just discovered by one of its reporters. It is doubtful if any story can be called new except in the qualified sense in which the detection of a hitherto unobserved comet is called the discovery of a new comet. All comets and all stories have existed during incalculable ages, and their regular reappearances do not justify us in assuming that they are new.

There is a vast difference in the periodic time of different stories, and it is probable that some of them revisit the earth not oftener than once in many millions of years. There is the story of "Bridget and the Unpremeditated Cat," which appeared in the year 1794, but of which no previous or subsequent observation has ever been made. The periodic time of this improving and retractile anecdote is at least six thousand years, and may, for all we know, be six or sixty million. There is a lamentable want of data in regard to the revolution of stories, but from such imperfect data as are accessible we can predict with much confidence the reappearance of several prominent stories. The one which appeared in the Chicago paper will, of course—if its time has been accurately computed—reappear in 1902, when it will suddenly dawn upon a score of simultaneous newspapers, all of which will hail it as a genuine

novelty. Vastly longer is the period of the story
of the man who, with the aid of his father, a
widow, and the widow's daughter, and an intricate
system of intermarriage, became his own grandfather. The first recorded appearance of this is
in a Sanscrit work, translated by BURTON, the
African explorer. Its second appearance was in
this city, in 1857, when it was told with much
applause at a negro minstrel entertainment. Between these two appearances there was an interval
of not far from 3,800 years. We need, therefore,
fear no recurrence of the story until about the
year 5650; a fact upon which we may fairly
congratulate ourselves, in view of its almost
unique tediousness and intricacy. In contrast
with the long cycle through which the grandfather
story sweeps, is the brief period of the anecdote
of the Irishman who thought that he would never
be able to put on a pair of tight boots without
previously wearing them for a day or two. This
reappears every two years with unvarying regu-
larity, and though it has been slightly modified

since the date when the sandal expanded into the boot, it has maintained the same period for at least 3,000 years.

It would be impossible, within moderate limits, to discuss the causes which first set stories in motion and regulated them by law. Neither can the perturbations and phases which certain stories manifest, nor the disturbing influence which one sometimes exerts upon another, be more than barely alluded to at this time. Very little observation is, however, needed to establish the fact that every story has its periodic time, and that its path and its speed are governed by natural and inflexible laws, as truly as are the path and speed of the moon, or the British drum-beat.

THE TOMBIGBEE INCIDENT.

THE LATEST CASE OF "HAZING."

"HAZING" has of late become altogether too frequent—as the *Herald* often remarks of murder and other atrocious crimes. At several of our leading colleges unhappy Freshmen have lately been "hazed," much to their astonishment and dissatisfaction. Bad as hazing is when it is perpetrated by boys, it is infinitely worse when young ladies are the "hazers." Their little hands were never made to pull each other's hair down, and that they should take part in scenes of riot and violence is particularly revolting to our nobler instincts. Nevertheless we must expect that the students of female colleges will emulate the practices of the students of male colleges, and we need not be surprised to learn that a peculiarly atrocious case of hazing recently occurred at a female college the name of which shall, from obvious motives, be suppressed.

Among the Freshwomen of this nameless college was one who possessed an unusually independent spirit, and refused to humble herself before the haughty Sophomoresses. Although the latter had forbidden Freshwomen to wear ribbons, or to bang their hair, she openly fluttered the showiest ribbons, and flaunted the most tightly-crimped bang in the faces of her natural superiors. Moreover, she wore a seal-skin sack—a garment which, by prescription, had become the badge of the upper-class women—and being an intrinsically pretty girl, she attracted a degree of attention when within sight of young men which was construed as a personal insult to the older students. There is no doubt that in these and other ways she not only exasperated the Sophomoresses, but formed a sort of nucleus around which other mutinous Freshwomen might be expected to gather.

About 12 o'clock on the night of the 23d of March ,last the independent Freshwoman was aroused by a gentle knock at her door. On demanding who was there, the reply was made, "It's me, dear; I've got a letter for you from a young man." In her excitement she did not pause to consider the essential improbability of this reply, but hastily unlocked the door. Instantly seven girls rushed into the room, locked the door behind them, and seizing the unhappy Freshwoman, gagged her with a "puff," and bound her hand and foot with two of her own sashes. This done, she was placed in a chair, and forbidden to move a muscle under pain of having a live mouse, which one of the aggressors had brought in a small box, let loose on the floor.

Such a threat would have curdled the blood in the veins of most girls, but this girl was made of firmer material, and, instead of fainting, she sat perfectly still and watched the "hazers." The latter were led by one of the most riotous students of the college, a girl who had repeatedly made surreptitious tea in her own room after bed-time, and had more than once been known to wave her handkerchief at casual young men. The whole party had prepared themselves for their lawless work by leaving their overskirts and their back hair in their rooms. They were evidently already under the influence of green tea, and they constantly made use of such revolting expressions as " my gracious," " my goodness me," and other equally shocking blasphemies. They had brought with them two quart bottles of cold tea, a supply of dry toast, and a jar of jelly. Seating themselves around the table, they rapidly consumed these intoxicating refreshments, and the helpless Freshwoman's heart sank within her as she perceived that they were deliberately stimulating themselves to a height of recklessness which would fit them for the most atrocious outrages.

For half an hour the revelers drank the fiery green tea, and made the midnight air ring with the rollicking songs of Messrs. MOODY and SANKEY. At length the leader judged that her companions were ripe for any sort of crime, and thereupon summoned them to carry out their nefarious design. They began by taking out and confiscating their victim's crimping-pins. They then carefully cut off with a pair of sharp scissors every vestige of her bang, leaving in its place a short stubble that closely resembled a masculine beard of three days' growth. The entire contents of the victim's own bottle of bandoline was then emptied upon her head, and her hair, after being combed straight back from her forehead, was secured in that position by a circular comb. Every particle of ribbon in her possession was seized by the "hazers," who, in cruel mockery of her fondness for ribbons of becoming tints, proceeded to trim all her dresses with a hideous particolored red and yellow ribbon. All this time the victim of these outrages made no sound, although the powder with which the "puff" was filled was several times on the point of choking her. When the "hazers" had finished their loathsome work they removed the gag, and forced the Freshwoman to solemnly promise on a volume of Emerson's Essays to wear only red and yellow ribbons, to send her seal-skin sack home by express, and to henceforth wear her hair in the simple and excessively unbecoming fashion in which they had arranged it.

Probably she would have refused at any cost to make such a promise had she not caught sight of herself in the mirror and thus sustained a shock which completely unnerved her.

It remains to be seen whether the college authorities will permit this brutal assault upon a defenseless student to remain unpunished ; or whether the spirit of " hazing " is to be permitted to spread among our female colleges, ruining the ribbons and obliterating the bangs of innocent Freshwomen.

THE END.

G. P. PUTNAM'S SONS have in preparation a series of volumes, to be issued under the title of

CURRENT DISCUSSION,

A COLLECTION FROM THE CHIEF ENGLISH ESSAYS ON QUESTIONS

OF THE TIME.

The series will be edited by EDWARD L. BURLINGAME, and is designed to bring together, for the convenience of readers and for a lasting place in the library, those important and representative papers from recent English periodicals, which may fairly be said to form the best history of the thought and investigation of the last few years. It is characteristic of recent thought and science, that a much larger proportion than ever before of their most important work has appeared in the form of contributions to reviews and magazines ; the thinkers of the day submitting their results at once to the great public, which is easiest reached in this way, and holding their discussions before a large audience, rather than in the old form of monographs reaching the special student only. As a consequence there are subjects of the deepest present and permanent interest, almost all of whose literature exists only in the shape of detached papers, individually so famous that their topics and opinions are in everybody's mouth —yet collectively only accessible, for re-reading and comparison, to those who have carefully preserved them, or who are painstaking enough to study long files of periodicals.

In so collecting these separate papers as to give the reader a fair if not complete view of the discussions in which they form a part ; to make them convenient for reference in the future progress of those discussions ; and especially to enable them to be preserved as an important part of the history of modern thought,—it is believed that this series will do a service that will be widely appreciated.

Such papers naturally include three classes :—those which by their originality have recently led discussion into altogether new channels ; those which have attracted deserved attention as powerful special pleas upon one side or the other in great current questions ; and finally, purely critical and analytical dissertations. The series will aim to include the best representatives of each of these classes of expression.

It is designed to arrange the essays included in the Series under such general divisions as the following, to each of which one or more volumes will be devoted :—

INTERNATIONAL POLITICS,   NATURAL SCIENCE,

RECENT ARCHÆOLOGICAL DISCOVERY,

QUESTIONS OF BELIEF,

ECONOMICAL AND SOCIAL SCIENCE,

HISTORY AND BIOGRAPHY,   LITERARY TOPICS.

Among the material selected for the first volume (International Politics), which will be issued immediately, are the following papers :

ARCHIBALD FORBES'S Essay on "THE RUSSIANS, TURKS, AND BULGARIANS;" Vsct. STRATFORD DE REDCLIFFE'S "TURKEY;" Mr. GLADSTONE'S "MONTENEGRO;" Professor GOLDWIN SMITH'S Paper on "THE POLITICAL DESTINY OF CANADA," and his Essay called "THE SLAVEHOLDER AND THE TURK;" Professor BLACKIE'S "PRUSSIA IN THE NINETEENTH CENTURY;" EDWARD DICEY'S "FUTURE OF EGYPT;" LOUIS KOSSUTH'S "WHAT IS IN STORE FOR EUROPE;" and Professor FREEMAN'S "RELATION OF THE ENGLISH PEOPLE TO THE WAR."

Among the contents of the second volume (Questions of Belief), are :

The two well-known "MODERN SYMPOSIA;" the Discussion by Professor HUXLEY, Mr. HUTTON, Sir J. F. STEPHEN, Lord SELBORNE, JAMES MARTINEAU, FREDERIC HARRISON, the DEAN OF ST. PAUL'S, the DUKE OF ARGYLL, and others, on "THE INFLUENCE UPON MORALITY OF A DECLINE IN A RELIGIOUS BELIEF;" and the Discussion by HUXLEY, HUTTON, Lord BLATCHFORD, the Hon. RODEN NOEL, Lord SELBORNE, Canon BARRY, GREG, the Rev. BALDWIN BROWN, FREDERIC HARRISON, and others, on "THE SOUL AND FUTURE LIFE. Also, Professor CALDERWOOD'S "ETHICAL ASPECTS OF THE DEVELOPMENT THEORY;" Mr. G. H. LEWES'S Paper on "THE COURSE OF MODERN THOUGHT;" THOMAS HUGHES on "THE CONDITION AND PROSPECTS OF THE CHURCH OF ENGLAND;" W. H. MALLOCK'S "IS LIFE WORTH LIVING?" FREDERIC HARRISON'S "THE SOUL AND FUTURE LIFE;" and the Rev. R. F. LITTLEDALE'S "THE PANTHEISTIC FACTOR IN CHRISTIAN THOUGHT."

The volumes will be printed in a handsome crown octavo form, and will sell for about $1 50 each.

G. P. PUTNAM'S SONS, 182 Fifth Avenue, New York.

CONSTANTINOPLE. By EDMUNDO DE AMICIS, author of "A Journey through Holland," "Spain and the Spaniards," &c. Translated by CAROLINE TILTON. With introduction by Prof. VINCENZO BOTTA. Octavo, cloth.

A trustworthy and exceptionally vivid description of the city which, in the present reopening of the Eastern question, is attracting more attention than any other in the world. De Amicis is one of the strongest and most brilliant of the present generation of Italian writers, and this latest work from his pen, as well from the picturesqueness of its descriptions as for its skilful analysis of the traits and characteristics of the medley of races represented in the Türkish capital, possesses an exceptional interest and value.

THE GREEKS OF TO-DAY. By Hon. CHARLES K. TUCKERMAN, late Minister Resident of the U. S. at Athens. Third Edition. 12mo, cloth, ... $1.50

This work attracted special attention at the time of its publication, in 1872, as giving a trustworthy and interesting picture of life in Greece, and of the character and status of the modern Greek. At this time, when public attention is so generally directed towards the scheme of practically re-establishing a Greek empire and Greek supremacy in the East, it is thought that a new edition will prove of interest and service.

"The information contained in the volume is ample and various, and it cannot fail to hold a high rank among the authorities on modern Greece."—*N. Y. Tribune.*

"No one can read this book without having his interest greatly increased in this brave, brilliant, and in every way remarkable people."—*N. Y. Times.*

"We know of no book which so combines freshness and fullness of information."—*N. Y. Nation.*

ENGLAND; POLITICAL AND SOCIAL. By AUGUSTE LAUGEL. Translated by J. M. HART. 12mo, cloth, ... $1.50

"It is written with a tone of confidence and force of expression which captivate."—*Buffalo Commercial.*

"Affords a clear, distinct, and comprehensive view of the political institutions of England."—*N. Y. Nation.*

"Here, in every sense, is a charming book. * * * * So full of thought, that, like the best of Macaulay's Essays, it will bear reading more than once. * * * * We have rarely met with more picture-like descriptions of what seems to have dwelt most upon his mind—English landscape scenery and rural life."—*N. Y. World.*

THE SILVER COUNTRY; or, THE GREAT SOUTHWEST. A Review of the Mineral and other Wealth, with the attractions and material development of the former kingdom of New Spain, comprising Mexico and the territory ceded by Mexico to the United States in 1848 and 1853. By ALEXANDER D. ANDERSON. 8vo, cloth, with Hypsometric Map, ... $1.75

"Just at the present moment everything which affords reliable information on the question of silver, its uses and production, is of almost paramount interest."—*Washington National Republican.*

"A very useful book for those who wish to study the silver question in its fundamental feature."—*Chicago Journal.*

"The book will unquestionably become the authority on the subject of which it treats."—*St. Louis Republican.*

WORKS OF FICTION

PUBLISHED BY

G. P. PUTNAM'S SONS

New York.

THE HOME ENCYCLOPÆDIA of Biography, History, Literature, Chronology and Essential Facts: for Libraries, Teachers, Students, and family use. Comprehensive, compact, and convenient for reference. Comprised in two parts. Price in cloth, $9 50; in half morocco, $14 50; sold separately or together.

Part I.—**The World's Progress.** A Dictionary of Dates, being a Chronological and Alphabetical Record of all Essential Facts in the Progress of Society, from the beginning of History to August, 1877. With Chronological Tables, Biographical Index, and a Chart of History. By G. P. PUTNAM, A. M. Revised and continued by F. B. PERKINS. In one handsome octavo volume of 1,000 pages, half morocco, $7 00; cloth extra $4 50

Contents: The World's Progress, 1867–1877; The Same, 1851–1867; The Same from the Beginning of History to 1851. United States Treasury Statistics. Literary Chronology, arranged in tables: Hebrew, Greek, Latin and Italian, British, German, French, Spanish and Portuguese, Dutch, Swedish, Danish, Polish, Russian, Arabian, Persian and Turkish, American. Heathen Deities and Heroes and Heroines of Antiquity. Tabular views of Universal History. Biographical Index, General. The Same, Index of Artists. Schools of Painting in Chronological Tables.

"A more convenient and labor-saving machine than this excellent compilation can scarcely be found in any language."—*N. Y. Tribune.*
"The largest amount of information in the smallest possible compass."—*Buffalo Courier.*
"The best manual of the kind in the English language.—*Boston Courier.*
"Well-nigh indispensable to a large portion of the community."—*N. Y. Courier & Register.*
"Absolutely essential to every merchant, student, and professional man."—*Christian Enquirer.*
"It is worth ten times its price * * * It completely supplies my need."—*S. W. Riegart, Principal of High School, Lancaster, Pa.*

Part II.—**The Cyclopædia of Biography:** A Record of the Lives of Eminent Men. By PARKE GODWIN. New edition, revised and continued to August, 1877. Octavo, containing over 1,200 pages, half morocco, $7 50; cloth $5 00

The Publishers claim for this work that it presents an admirable combination of compactness and comprehensiveness. The previous editions have recommended themselves to the public favor, as well for the fulness of their lists of essential names, as for the accuracy of the material given. The present edition will, it is believed, be found still more satisfactory as to these points, and possesses for American readers the special advantage over similar English works, in the full proportion of space given to eminent American names.
"We can speak from long experience in the use of this book, as a well-thumbed copy of the first edition has lain for years on our library table for almost daily reference. A concise, compact, biographical dictionary is one of the most necessary and convenient manuals, and we seldom fail to find what we look for in this excellent compendium."—*Home Journal.*

FROTHINGHAM (OCTAVIUS BROOKS) **The Life of Gerrit Smith.** With portrait on Steel, and other illustrations. Octavo, cloth extra, (*In Press.*) . . . .

The life of one who was an earnest philanthropist, a devoted worker in the anti-slavery cause, and a clear-headed man of business, who had an active and important part to play in the history and development of his native State, and in the reform movements of the whole country. The volume is of moderate compass, and presents in an artistic narrative the story of a life of unique character and value.

MAZADE (CHARLES de) **The Life of Count Cavour.** Translated by GEO. MEREDITH. Octavo, cloth extra, . . $3 00

The life of Cavour is the record of the founding of the Kingdom of Italy, or rather of the forming of the Italian Nation. The biographer has brought to this work a hearty appreciation of and admiration for his subject, a full knowledge of the history of the time, and a terse, epigrammatic style; and the translation has been performed with taste and accuracy. The volume is alike indispensable to the student of modern history, and fascinating to the general reader.

PROCTOR (RICHARD A.) **The Myths and Marvels of Astronomy.** Octavo, cloth. $4 00

Mr. Proctor is always an interesting writer, and has taken for his present work a subject that under the dullest treatment would be fascinating reading. A large part of the volume is devoted to the Science of Astrology, which has itself produced a library of literature, and in the remaining chapters he discusses the long list of legends and marvels which the imagination of man has from time immemorial associated with the heavenly bodies.

SELECT BRITISH ESSAYISTS (The) A series planned to consist of half a dozen volumes, comprising the representative papers of *The Spectator, Tatler, Guardian, Rambler, Lounger, Mirror, Looker-On,* etc., etc. Edited, with Introduction and Biographical Sketches of the Authors, by JOHN HABBERTON.

Vol. I. THE SPECTATOR. By ADDISON and STEELE. Square. 16mo, cloth extra, ... $1 25

Vol. II.—SIR ROGER DE COVERLY PAPERS. From *The Spectator.* One volume, square, 16mo, cloth extra, ... $1 00

Vol. III.—THE TATLER. . . . .

"Mr. Habberton has given us a truly readable and delightful selection."—*Liberal Christian.*

"The series will doubtless tend to revive a more general interest in a class of works which, in spite of the standard character conceded to them, are now greatly neglected."—*N. Y. Tribune.*

VAN LAUN. The History of French Literature. By HENRI VAN LAUN, Translator of Taine's "History of English Literature," the Works of Molière, etc.

Vol. I.—FROM ITS ORIGIN TO THE RENAISSANCE. 8vo, cloth extra, $2 50.—Vol. II.—FROM THE RENAISSANCE TO THE CLOSE OF THE REIGN OF LOUIS XIV. 8vo, cloth extra, $2 50.—Vol. III.—FROM THE REIGN OF LOUIS XIV TO THAT OF NAPOLEON III. 8vo, cloth extra, $2 50.

The Set, three volumes, in box, half calf, $13 50, cloth extra, $7 50

"Mr. Van Laun has not given us a mere critical study of the works he considers, but has done his best to bring their authors, their way of life, and the ways of those around them, before us in a living likeness."—*London Daily News*

www.ingramcontent.com/pod-product-compliance
Lightning Source LLC
Chambersburg PA
CBHW030814020726
47499CB00006B/1915